Adalithiel

Andrea Rose Washington

D1409915

1

Acknowledgements

Writing this book was a hard decision for me, and I'm very thankful to everyone who supported me in this redo of my previous work, The Veiled Truth, and The Unraveling. Adalithiel was such a labor of love, and I am so proud of it. To everyone who bought The Veiled Truth and The Unraveling, you all get a special thank you for sticking with me until this book. Thank You to my friends and family who agreed to read many versions of this book before its completion! It was a lot, but you all helped me get here!

I love you all!

Prologue

She was done. Her time for living was over. No longer would she have to run and hide or live in fear. She accepted her fate; she would not beg them for her life. She would die with dignity and honor, the same honor they tried so hard to take from her. She lived her life the way she was raised. She was a good person, never lied, never stole and while this ending wasn't fair, she would accept it. She knew one day the truth would come out. If not today, then soon, the world would know of the great travesty that took place here.

Her cell door sprang open, and the guards glared down at her small battered frame. She was accustomed to their nightly visits, but she knew this one was different. They wanted to break her, but they had failed. Her spirit could not be broken. No matter how hard they tried, she would never allow herself to be broken. She would never admit defeat. They would never learn the location of her family. She would take that secret with her to the grave.

"Your time's up," one of the guards snarled, roughly grabbing her arms and hauling her to her feet and dragged her out of the cell. She didn't fight them but allowed them to take her to her death. They walked for a few minutes, and she realized they were taking her to the courtyard. They were going to make this a public execution.

As they reached the door, she took a deep breath and steeled her emotions. No tears would fall today. No one would get the satisfaction of seeing her break down. She needed to be strong for her family, to prove to them that this act was not stronger than they were. As the doors opened, she closed her eyes briefly, took another deep breath and walked out.

She kept her head held high as she was bombarded with taunts and screams from those who used to love her. People who used to look up to her, people she loved and cared about. They now spewed some of the most hateful words as she was led to the center of the courtyard where the guillotine stood.

She took a final look at the people

she was raised to love and protect. Her people. She let a small smile grace her face. Then she knelt, bowed her head, and found peace.

Chapter One

The cool breeze blew in giving Sasha a much-needed breath of cold air. She leaned back on her heels and wiped her brow admiring the beauty of the setting sun over the small mountain before surveying her work.

She had been picking strawberries all afternoon and filled three barrels. She stood up, brushed off her jeans, and took in the beauty of the farm. On the back of their property stood the barn that her mother let her paint when she was fifteen. There was a mural of their farm on one side, and a picture of her and her parents on the other. Next to the barn was their "mini-orchard," as she liked to call it. There were eight rows of trees; two apples, two oranges, two pears, and two cherries. In front of the orchard was a small cornfield, and next to that was their vegetable patch that held carrots, potatoes, zucchini, and squash. To the left, they also had the grapevine arbors and their tomato vine. The land where Sasha stood held strawberries, blueberries, raspberries, and blackberries. Their farm wasn't as big as some, but it was all that Sasha and her mother could handle on a daily basis since her father died when she was 10.

"Sasha!" a familiar voice yelled, pulling her out of her thoughts. Sasha looked up and smiled, seeing her best friend, Cassandra Lightworth, coming towards her.

"Hey, how's life on the farm?" Cassie joked, coming to a stop in front of her.

"Same as always," she shrugged. "Picking fruit to sell, to buy more seeds to plant, to grow, to sell. It's the never ending cycle of the farm, a cycle I wish was over for the day," she sighed, wiping her hands on her jeans.

"Well…" Cassie said with a sly look on her face and a wiggle of her fingers. "I could help you finish your work faster… I mean only if you are fine with it."

"I am completely fine with that. Help away!" Sasha laughed moving out of the way. Cassie raised her hand, made a slight weaving motion as her fingertips glowed a bright white.

It never mattered how many times she

saw Cassie perform magic; she was always awestruck. She took another step back twirling her necklace, a gift from her father. She watched the strawberries, encased in a white glow, snap off the vines and float to the waiting barrels. Cassie threw Sasha a wink as the last strawberry dropped.

"You know I love when you do that. You make my life so much easier," She laughed, and Cassie rolled her eyes. "Glad I can be of service."

"You should be! Otherwise, you would be wasting away." Sasha grabbed one of the barrels and started carrying it to the waiting cart. "Can you grab the other one for me, please?" she asked, hoisting the barrel onto the flatbed of the cart. Cassie nodded, grabbed the other barrel and loaded it on the flatbed. They locked up the back and Sasha climbed into the driver's seat as Cassie slid in next to her and they took off for the barn.

"Not that I'm not happy to see you, but why are you here? Isn't it family dinner time?" Sasha sped around a corner causing Cassie to grip her seat a little tighter.

"Oh, I thought I told you. My parents went out of town for their bi-yearly romantic getaway. They are gone for the next five days," Cassie grinned.

"Wait, you have the house to yourself. We have to throw a party!" Sasha gushed. "It's going to be epic!"

"Pump your brakes. The house is on total lockdown. Every neighbor is on watch. They even asked their Enforcer friend George to do a drive-by every night."

Sasha groaned. "I guess we blew their trust last time?"

Cassie laughed. "Who knew throwing a house party that ended in a couple of broken family heirlooms would make them so untrusting?"

"Well, you know my Mom would love to have you here for the week. She would hate for you to stay alone."

"Those were the words I was counting on," she smirked. "I already left my bags on your front steps."

Sasha pulled up next to the barn, hopped out, and grabbed one of the barrels out of the back while Cassie grabbed one too. They put them in the barn and grabbed the third barrel off the cart before Sasha locked up the barn. They climbed back in front of the cart and headed to the house.

Sasha's house was simple, only two stories but more than enough room for just Sasha and her mom. There was a red brick foundation on the house and weathered wood siding that worked its way up to the roof. The kitchen had a bay window allowing them to see down the road leading up to their house. Cassie's bags sat on the porch Sasha's father fixed after she fell through a broken beam when she was eight.

"Mom, I'm done, and Cassie's here," Sasha yelled as they lugged Cassie's bags into the house.

"I'm in the kitchen," Sasha's mother, Jasmine, called back.

Sasha shut the door behind them and started to take off her mud-caked boots. Her mother hated when she tracked dirt through the house. She opened the front closet and grabbed her house shoes, an old black and white striped pair of running shoes.

"Hey, Ms. Jasmine," Cassie called as she walked into the kitchen, followed by Sasha.

The kitchen had a nice homey feel to it. The wooden countertops and shelves were handmade by Sasha's father, Sam when he redid the kitchen. Her mother loved to cook and bake and wanted the perfect kitchen to aid her. Her father loved her mother, so he just went along with what she wanted. They had an old brown refrigerator that Jasmine refused to replace, even though Sasha had begged for years. They replaced the stove last year only because the one that came with the house broke down past the point of no return. Their new one wasn't even brand new, but it matched the brown color scheme her mother seemed to love so much.

Jasmine was standing by the stove, stirring what Sasha hoped was her famous chili. The rumble in her stomach hoped so as well. Jasmine, who was 37, didn't look a day over 25. Most people thought they were sisters, much to Sasha's dismay. Many people around town said Sasha looked like her mother, but she didn't see it. She had her mother's bright brown eyes that changed in the sunlight. They shared the same long brown curly hair that both women preferred to keep up in a ponytail or a bun. Neither liked dealing with their hair when it was down, as it had the tendency to frizz up on them. Sasha also received her caramel skin tone from her mother. But that was all the resemblance she could see to her mom or her late father. They explained when she was younger, she received her bone structure, nose, and lips from her father's mother, and since she never met her, she could only agree with what she was told.

"Hi Cassie, it's nice to see you as always. Though I have to wonder, are you the reason my daughter finished her work far too fast?" Jasmine smiled at the two girls.

Cassie blanched and worked to come up with an excuse. "I have no idea what you are talking about; I just got here as Sasha pulled up to the house."

"Oh," Jasmine sounded surprised. "You just got here when Sasha finished." Jasmine mulled over. "Well then, that's a whole different story." She murmured. "I guess what I am having a hard time trying to figure out is, if you just got here, who did I see outside talking to Sasha while finishing her work? Do you girls see my dilemma, something is not adding up?"

"Mom..." Sasha tried.

"I know you are not about to *Mom* me young lady. You know the rules. I have told you too many times that Cassie cannot help you using her powers," Jasmine snapped.

"What's the big deal," Sasha complained. "You wanted the work done, and now it is. Why does it matter how? It was easier to do it this way."

"If I wanted to use magic I would hire magicals to come do the job for me. You might not always have help, Sasha. I want you to be able to rely on yourself. You need to learn that you cannot always take the easy way out because one day there won't be."

Sasha felt her cheeks flush in embarrassment at being reprimanded in front of Cassie. "Sorry Mom," she whispered.

"I offered the help! Sasha never asked me." Cassie blurted, trying to defend her friend.

Jasmine stared at the girls before letting a smile grace her lips. "Just please don't let it happen again, okay? Cassie, if you want to help that's fine, just no magic."

"Yes, Ma'am," both girls agreed.

"Okay, so on a lighter note," Jasmine said, trying to ease the tension. "Are you girls hungry? Dinner is done." She turned off the stove and reached for the bowls, but the sound of the doorbell stopped her.

"Are we expecting anyone?" Sasha looked at her.

"No, and I didn't see anyone walk up." Jasmine headed to the door as another knock rang through the house.

"Hello?" she called through the door.

"Hello," came an unfamiliar out of breath voice. "I am so happy you're home! Hi, Ma'am... um, my car died on me down the road I was wondering if I could use your phone to call a tow truck. My cell is dead, and I've been out here for hours."

Jasmine looked back at Sasha and Cassie placing a finger over her lips motioning them to be silent.

"On this road?" she questioned.

"Yeah, I was on my way out of town when it just died on me. I know just my luck, but if you just let me use your phone that would be amazing." He continued.

"This road won't take you out of town," Jasmine said.

"Yeah, I realize that now," he gave a humorless laugh from his side of the door, "I got turned around out there, it's been a whole ordeal, I'm just ready to leave...if you could just let me in so I can use your phone..."

"And you walked up the front to get here?" she asked cutting him off.

"Yes."

"I was just standing in front of my window before you knocked on the door. I never saw you walk up the road," she said.

"Um…" he struggled to find the right words.

"Leave," Jasmine ordered before he could find a new excuse.

"Ma'am please just let me use your phone." He insisted.

"I said to leave!" She said a bit more forceful.

"Open the door." His voice had lost its pleasant tone. The door handle started to shake, and Sasha grabbed Cassie's hand backing away from the door.

"Leave now, and I will forget you were ever here." Jasmine reached over to the alarm panel and typed in a code Sasha had never seen before.

"Open the door!" the man started banging. "Don't make this harder than it needs to be!"

"This is your last chance to leave." Jasmine pressed the last button and took a step back.

"Mom?" Sasha asked as a yellow light emitted from the alarm panel and spread across the walls.

"We need to hurry; we don't have much time." Jasmine explained as sounds of small explosion sounded around the house, "The shield will only keep them out for so long, we need to move while we still can."

Sasha ran to the window pulling back the shade a bit. A red stream of energy hit the glass, the force knocking her back a few feet.

She ducked as another ball of energy broke through the window and shards of glass rained over her. The dark green couch exploded in white hot flames as the fire consumed it.

She chanced another peek out the open hole - there were at least three men she could see heading for her house. They formed more red energy balls and fired them at the house.

"Sasha duck!" Cassie screamed.

Sasha dropped down and turned her head to see Cassie send a bright yellow ball of energy out over her head. It expanded outside the house taking the initial impact, but it wasn't strong enough to stop all the attacks; both girls were thrown across the room hitting the wall behind them hard.

Sasha's eyes widen watching her mother create small orange energy balls in her hand. She sent them out the opening, and multiple small explosions followed.

"Mom?" she asked.

Another energy ball blasted into the living room setting it ablaze. A strong flame started making its way up the mantle that held every family photo they had left of her father, Sam. Sasha scrambled up to her feet and went for the photos, but Jasmine tackled her back to the ground as another orange energy ball soared over them.

Jasmine glanced out the hole in her living room wall and saw five men dressed in black. They were almost blending into the oncoming darkness, making their way towards the house. The man in the middle raised his arm, and a bright orange energy ball appeared.

"Get down!" Jasmine yelled at Sasha who wiggled out of her grasp and rushed to the pictures. Cassie grabbed Sasha and pulled her down as the energy ball exploded in the room. Sasha hit the floor hard, banging her head on her necklace shattering the jewel held within. She blinked her eyes as she tried to pull them into focus. Her heart thumped rushing her blood through her body like never before. She shut her eyes to stop her head from spinning and tried to focus on one thought. She squinted her eyes and looked to her left. Cassie was lying next to her. Her mouth was moving, but she couldn't make out the words. Sasha turned back to her mother, she was yelling at her, but she couldn't make out the words, it was like the world was moving in slow motion.

She pulled herself to her knees ignoring Cassie attempts to pull her back to the ground. She stood on shaky feet as sections of the house fell around her. She turned back to the mantel. Most of the pictures were going up in flames. There was one left, hanging above the rest not yet touched by the flames. She watched in slow motion as the flames jumped up towards the photo, desperate to consume it. One thought crossed her mind. *She would not lose that photo.*

She glanced out the opening. The men were about to enter the house. She didn't have a thought just the urge to force them away. "No!" she screamed as her body glowed a bright blue. Power surged through her like blood rushing through her veins. She felt alive. Energy shot from her hands like a canon, and it hit the men, sending them back into the woods.

She turned back to the mantel, raised her arm, and grabbed the flame covered picture. She brushed the remaining flames off and rested her hand on the mantel. Energy left her body and spread across the mantel extinguishing the flames as they reached them. The three women watched as the blue light raced around the room putting out all the flames.

"Sasha," Cassie stared in awe at the room now devoid of flames. "What did you do?" She had never seen a display of power this strong before. "How did you do it?"

Sasha didn't answer; she only focused on the saved photo. She turned to her mother, whose face was etched with horror and fear.

"What happened to your necklace?" Jasmine whispered, her eyes locked on Sasha's neck where the ruined necklace laid. Sasha's hand instinctively flew to her neck in search of the now broken piece of jewelry. Before she could answer, voices from outside startled them. Those men were up and coming back. *I might have saved the picture, but we are still going to die*, Sasha thought as she pocketed the photo.

"We need to get to the basement," Jasmine ordered, pulling them towards the charred door under the stairs.

"We don't have a basement!" Sasha looked around the charred room.

"Yes we do, I just never told you." Jasmine jerked the door open. She took the box of books out and pulled opened a latch that until now Sasha had never noticed. "Hurry up and get down there," Jasmine ordered.

Sasha glanced down the opening to the small staircase. She descended, then Cassie and Jasmine followed behind her. Jasmine pulled the latch closed and pressed her hand to the underside. A green light engulfed it then faded. Sasha heard a slight thump on top of the latch and guessed the books were back on top. Hopefully, this would buy them the time they needed.

Sasha took in the basement that her mother was currently running around. She was grabbing items from around the room and stuffed them in a bag. There wasn't much to it. It was simple, the walls painted white, and there was a desk with a few books, papers, and a couple of trunks around the room.

"Mom!" Sasha whispered, but Jasmine placed her finger over her lips. She signaled her not to talk then she motioned to the ceiling.

They are in the house, Sasha realized as she shrunk back against the wall.

"Where are they?" A deep male voice yelled above them. "Search the house!" Jasmine, Sasha, and Cassie stared at the ceiling, listening to the men toss the house. Sasha froze when they started tearing through the house.

"They are not here!" a different voice yelled.

"There's no way they could have gotten past us. We had the house surrounded," the first voice shouted back.

They stared up at the ceiling as the men walked across the floor above them.

"What do we do now?" Sasha whispered to her mother, never taking her eyes off the ceiling.

"*We* don't do anything," Jasmine stressed. "*You two* are going to get out and leave. I am going to hold them off to give you guys time to escape," she explained, thrusting a duffle bag into each of the girl's hands. She ran back to the desk and grabbed a journal from the top drawer of the desk and handed it to Sasha.

"Wait," Sasha shook her head. "What do you mean you are going to hold them off? You can't stay here. They'll kill you! You have to come with us."

"I have to. Otherwise they will catch up. You need time to get away. I'm so sorry Sasha, I never wanted you to find out this way," Jasmine pulled her into a tight hug and kissed her forehead as she pulled back then pulled Cassie into a hug as well. "Everything you two need is in this journal. Use it to get out of town get to the safe point, don't trust anyone until you get there."

"Why can't we just go to the Enforcers?" Cassie asked in a hushed voice.

"It's not safe there," Jasmine rushed out. "Who's after me…us...has a lot of power; you need to stay underground!" she pressed as the sound of the men upstairs grew louder. "Someone in this town had to give us away. I made sure that we are not on any record in the government. Someone had to tell them where we are. Now follow the instructions in this book, and you will be safe." Jasmine walked over to the far wall and ran her hand over a panel letting dark green energy cover the wall panel. It faded after a revealing an opening to a dark tunnel.

"There's a hidden door under here," a gruff voice yelled from above them, causing a collective chill to run down their spines.

Jasmine pulled the two girls over and forced them through the open door. "Follow the instructions in the book. Remember – second, first, third, 20 steps then push to the right. Then go to the river," she explained, as the men began banging on the door above.

"Mom, what are you talking about? You have to come with us," Sasha pleaded.

"Honey" she said, cupping Sasha's face in her hands as the pounding grew louder. "I love so much," Jasmine sniffed as the sound of wood break filled the air. "But I need you and Cassie to leave now! Remember, second, first, third, 20 steps and push to the right then head to the river." Jasmine pushed the girls through the opening again and closed it as the basement door gave way.

"What? No, Mom!" Sasha banged on the wall the sounds of her mother's fight ranged through the tunnel panel.

"Sasha, stop!" Cassie wrapped her arms around her. "You need to stop! If you keep that up, they'll hear you! You have to calm down."

"No!" She struggled to get free. "She is all I have left!" She cried

"Sasha, we have to go. She told us to leave." Cassie started to drag Sasha from the tunnel door. "If they get to us they will kill us. We need to leave; we can't help her if we're dead."

Sasha wriggled out of Cassie's hold and sunk to the ground. "No..." she sobbed into her hand.

"Sasha." Cassie fell to her knees next to her wrapping her arms around her.

Both teens sat in silence listening to Jasmine fight for them on the other side of the wall.

She waited a minute then nodded to Cassie. Together they stood grabbed their bags and started down the hall. Sasha gave one last look over her shoulder as she stuffed the journal in her bag. *I'm going to save you, Mom... I promise,* she thought, as they started to run down the tunnel.

Chapter Two

Sasha huffed as they ran down the tunnel. It was cold, dark, and seemed to go on forever. *How long has this been here? How long has she been planning this?* Sasha wondered, as they finally came to an opening but were faced with two new tunnels.

"What?" Cassie huffed coming up next to her. "Which one do we go down?" Cassie looked between the two tunnels.

"I am not sure," Sasha shook her head.

"What did your mom tell you before she closed the door? It was a couple of numbers."

Sasha closed her eyes and tried to remember the last few words she heard from her mother. "Second, first, third, 20 steps and push to the right, then the river," Sasha recited.

"She had to be talking about the tunnels," Cassie guessed. "So second tunnel?"

"Yeah," Sasha readily agreed, and they headed down the second tunnel from the left. After a few minutes, they came to another opening to four more tunnels. Without hesitation, Sasha headed down the first tunnel with Cassie behind her.

This tunnel was a bit longer than the last two, and the gap between Cassie and Sasha grew. "Wait!" Cassie finally begged as she slowed down and leaned on the wall to catch her breath. Sasha turned and jogged back to her.

Sasha worked to slow her breathing like her father always taught her. "What's wrong?"

"I am not used to running like this. My legs feel like jelly," Cassie wheezed dropping her bag to the ground.

"Slow your breathing, take longer, deeper breaths," Sasha instructed, showing her how to do it.

"We are all not natural born runners like you," Cassie laughed trying to ease the tension. Sasha smiled and leaned on the wall as well using this to catch her breath along with her. For a few minutes, all that was heard was the rhythmic sounds of the two girls breathing.

Finally, Sasha pushed off the wall and grabbed her bag off the ground. "Are you ready to go again?"

Cassie nodded and pushed off the wall as well. "As I'll ever be, I just want to get out of the tunnel."

"I agree, it's creepy down here." Sasha shook her head as strong vibration shook the tunnel walls sending a light shower of dirt down on them.

"What was that?" Cassie shook the loose dirt from her hair.

"It's like something is banging on the outside wall." Cassie guessed.

Sasha gasped "It's them, they are trying to get in. We need to get going!" She grabbed Cassie's arm and started down the tunnel again.

The vibrations grew stronger and more frequent until it was a constant force. The men were getting closer to getting in, and they needed to be out of the tunnel before that happened.

They found themselves at another junction with three more tunnel openings. A loud explosion rattled the walls, the force sending the girls to their knees.

"They got in." Sasha gasped scrambling

to her feet, pulling Cassie along with her. "We need to keep going." They ran down the third tunnel and started counting off steps. The explosion dislodged dirt and rocks. If they did not get out of the tunnel soon, they were going to be buried alive before the men even reached them.

As soon as she hit 20, Sasha skidded to a stop. "We took the twenty steps; the exit should be here to the right." She turned in a circle. "But we are still in the middle of the tunnel."

"The exit has to be here," Cassie paced. "We just have to find it!"

"Where? We're still in the middle of the tunnel." Sasha felt along the wall.

"It has to be like the entrance to the tunnel." Cassie guessed. "One section will let us out."

They ran their hands across the walls looking for the exit. "Where do you think it will be?"

"I wish I knew," Sasha asked and pushed, but there was no give. "If it is like the entrance, we might need a spell to open it. Mom did."

"You're right." Cassie took a step back and held out her hand. A dark green light

left her hand and ran across the wall.
"There," she pointed to the section Sasha
was about to push. "The opening is there.
But it won't open for me."

"What do you mean it won't?"

"Your Mom must have sealed it so only
she could open it," Cassie explained.

"That makes no sense. She would not
send us down here without a way out. You
have to be able to open it."

"I'm telling you I can't. It won't work for
me. But maybe it will work for you."

"What?"

"You have powers, you used them in the
house, if your Mom sealed this so only she
could open it, you should be able to. You are
her daughter."

Sasha shook her head. "Cassie I have no
idea how I did what I did in the house. It just
happened, and I doubt you have time to
teach me right now."

"Well... ok I have another idea," Cassie
assured. "Come here." Sasha walked over to
her. Now raise your hand like this," she
instructed, and Sasha copied. "Ok...
normally I would never do this, but since
you have powers, it should work."

"What should work?"

"Me running my powers through you."

"I'm sorry what." She turned to her.

"I'll explain later just keep your hand up." Cassie stood behind Sasha, and her hands glowed dark green once more. The energy shot from her hand and ran up Sasha's arm and hit the door opening it.

"Wow," Sasha said. "That felt weird. So weird."

"Yeah..." Cassie stared at Sasha.

"What?" She asked as they walked out into the dark forest. "Why are you looking at me like that?"

"We need to seal the door." She said ignoring Sasha's question. "Same way as before."

"Ok." Sasha got back into position and Cassie closed the door through her.

"Sasha." Cassie started. "You're powerful."

"What? No," Sasha shook her head. "I'm not."

"Yes, you are." Cassie nodded. "I've never felt power like that before."

"What are you talking about?"

"You're like a battery.... you should be wiped out from what you did in the house, but you're not. When I ran my power through you, it grew...like tenfold. Why would your mother keep that from you?"

"From the looks of it, she's kept a lot from me," Sasha muttered. "And anyway we need to keep going."

"Where to?" Cassie asked looking around the dark forest.

"The river. That was the last thing she said to remember."

"How do we get there?" Cassie looked around the woods. "We are in the middle of the forest. Which way is the river."

Sasha looked around the forest trying to figure out where they were. "I think I know where we are," she said after a moment, "I used to go camping out here all the time when I was younger before my dad died. I thought they just wanted me to know the land where I was living. Now I feel like they just wanted me to know just in case this ever happens, which makes me wonder how long have they been expecting this?"

"They tried to prepare you. Sasha…" Cassie reached out, but Sasha waved her off.

"To prepare me they would have had to actually tell me what is going on," Sasha uttered. "I have no idea who took my mother, why they took her or where. My mother is magical, and so am I, but do they tell me? No! Do they show me how to use these powers, how to control them? No! My life!" She ran her hand through her hair in a fit a rage then sunk to her knees. "My Mom," she sobbed, and Cassie came next to her hugging her close, "But it doesn't matter," Sasha wiped her eyes with the back of her hands and pushed to her feet. "We are stuck here in the middle of the forest, and we need to keep going. My mom said the river, and I know how to get there."

"Lead the way," Cassie said.

Sasha took the lead and Cassie followed close behind. Together they went deeper into the forest than Cassie ever wished to travel.

They walked for ten minutes until they started to hear the soft sounds of rushing water.

"We are getting closer," Sasha mentioned. Cassie nodded but did not speak up. The sound of rushing water took over as they broke through the clearing.

"It's just a shack," Sasha said staring at the small dark building. "Are we supposed to hide out in a shack in the middle of the woods? It looks like it's about to fall apart."

She commented on the broken windows and sliding shingles.

"Well, we will never know if we don't check it out?" Cassie suggested opening the door heading inside. "The outside does not match the inside."

"No, it does not," Sasha said walking in behind her. The inside of the shack was set up like a state of the art garage. There was an older jeep sitting in the middle of the room. Next to it looked like a couple of extra tanks of gas and a few more trunks.

"I guess we are to drive to wherever she has planned for us to go?" Cassie said checking out the jeep then slipping into the passenger seat.

"I guess," Sasha slid into the driver seat. "But where? She said don't trust anyone"

"She did give you that journal," Cassie suggested. "The answer has to be in there."

"It would be easier if she just came with us." Sasha quipped as she rummaged through her bag. She pulled out the journal and started to look for answers. "Wow," she muttered after a moment of reading.

"What is it?"

"It's in our code..." she whispered.

"Code?" Cassie asked.

"When I was younger and learning how to write, I came up with my own words. My Mom thought it was pretty adorable, so she had me teach her and Dad. Over the years we grew the language, and we would have full conversations with it. It was our little secret. But it's been years since we've used it, I can't believe she remembered it."

"I bet she wanted to make sure only you could read this if anyone else found the journal."

"I don't know if I remember everything. It's been years since I've even thought about this. Sasha skimmed through the first couple of pages

"But you can remember it...right? I mean it's the only way we can get to where we will be safe."

"I think so..." she turned the page, "...a safe point," she read. "My Mom mentions something about a safe point and then a couple of numbers too short to be a phone number."

"Well," Cassie opened the glove compartment and rummaged around. "I found a map ....with Longitude and Latitude numbers on it. Maybe that's what the numbers are?" Cassie guessed.

"No," Sasha shook her head. "They're not long enough."

"Well...maybe it is another code." Cassie started to look around the glove compartment again. She pulled out a small compact screen. "Maybe for this." She handed it over to Sasha.

"It looks like a GPS, but it's too small." She pressed the on the button. The small screen emitted a beep and flickered on. They waited as the little machine booted up.

"Enter destination?" Sasha read. She typed in the number from the journal and waited for the GPS to connect.

"You have got to be kidding me..." Cassie stared at the screen. "These coordinates are across the country. That's like at least a two day's journey."

"I've never been out of this town before," Sasha admitted.

"Neither have I."

"I don't think we will be able to stop along the way. It's not like we can check into a hotel."

"Well, it looks like she packed everything we would need." Cassie looked through her pack. "I have a couple changes of clothes. Three boxes of granola bars, a couple packs of dried fruit and one, two, looks like four bottles of water."

"Looks like I have the same." Sasha looked through hers. "And," she started up the jeep, "it looks like we have a full tank of gas."

"Plus, the two extra tanks," Cassie added.

"Looks like we have enough to make it. She planned it all out." Sasha got out of the jeep, grabbed the tanks and loaded them on to the trunk. She checked the other trunks lying around the room and found a few more bottles of water and more dried fruit. "I guess this was just in case we could not leave through the basement."

She climbed back into the driver's seat, and Cassie mounted the small screen to the dashboard. Sasha clicked the garage opener.

With one last glance to each other Sasha hit the gas and took off into the back roads of the darkening forest. Off to what they hoped was safety.

Chapter Three

The men stood outside the burnt remains of the Delant house. Each was clad in solid black from head to toe. The first was about six feet tall, and a little on the hefty side. He stood slightly apart from the others, shifting his weight from one foot to the other. The second man stood a short 5'5", but his clothing fit to utter perfection. He made sure that what he lacked in height, he made up in strength. The third man stood in the middle, and at 6'4", was the tallest, with broad shoulders and a trim waist. The fourth and fifth men had oddly similar bodies, both 6'2" and of medium build. From behind, they were often mistaken for twins. At their feet an unconscious Jasmine, her wrists, and feet bound together. Her mouth gagged and around her neck was a bright gold necklace like the one Sasha wore. They were not able to search the tunnels for the missing girls. In their hurry to get in, they caused a number of the tunnels to cave in.

"Boss…" the second man said to the third, "We should get out of here before someone comes to visit this place."

"Visit?" the fourth man scoffed. "Who would visit this late in the evening? It's time for this sleepy little town to go to bed. We've watched this house all week, listened to all the phone calls, no one is coming here for a while. We could hang out here all night if we wanted to," he laughed.

"That's what we thought, and the other little girl showed up. We shouldn't risk it," the second guy reasoned.

"Squirt, just chill out. Stressing will stunt your growth – well, stunt it more…" the fourth guy laughed at his own joke.

The boss rolled his eyes at his men before clearing his throat to gain their attention. "He's right. We need to move. Just because there was nothing planned, doesn't mean they won't get a visitor. We lost the other one, and we have another witness; we cannot afford the risk of anyone showing up and losing her." He kicked at Jasmine's feet.

"What do we tell them about the other two?" the second man questioned.

"The truth – they escaped. To where, I

have no idea, but we have her, and we can let them get the rest of the information out of her."

"We still get paid the full amount, right?" the fifth man asked. He never cared what the job was, as long as it paid well.

"I doubt it, but we got the one they truly wanted. The other one is not as important." he reached down and picked up Jasmine and threw her over his shoulder like she weighed nothing.

The sound of an approaching car's engine set them on edge; they would not be alone for much longer. They disappeared into the shadows of the forest. Bright beams of the car's headlights illuminated the road.

The driver, Susan Comesto, was a beautiful woman. She had striking ice-blue eyes and short wavy brown hair just a shade darker than her sun-kissed skin. She slammed on her breaks at the sight of the house.

It was gone… the house was gone; burned to the ground. Only the bones – the beams and foundation – remained.

"What happened?" she gasped climbing out of the car and took a few steps forward. "Jasmine! Sasha!" she called into the darkness. "Guys are you out there?" she walked up to the steps and scanned the area, but in this darkness, there was no way she was ever going to see anything. She ran back into her car jumped in, pulled out her phone, and called for the Enforcers.

It took five long minutes for three Enforcer cars and one Fire Control truck to drive up the long driveway. They slammed on their breaks seeing the state of the house. The members exited their cars; their faces fixed on the destroyed Delant Home. They made their way past Susan and started to check out the home.

Susan exited her car once she saw Robert Walsh, Head Enforcer of the small town of Blanton, climbed out of his car.

"What happened?" he asked once he reached her. His Enforcers headed straight for the house to set up the perimeter.

"I don't know," she shook her head. "I just got here; I spoke to Jasmine earlier today. She invited me over for dinner...but I didn't think I would make it; I was busy finishing a deadline for work."

"But you decided to come anyway?" he questioned.

"I finished earlier than expected so I

figured I would come by for a bit to hang out. It's the weekend, so no need to wake up early tomorrow, but I got here to this," she gestured to the ruined house.

"Did you see any smoke on your drive up here?"

"She wouldn't have." Fred Johnson, a seasoned Fire Control member, joined them.

"Excuse me if I'm wrong but the house burned to the ground, there would have been huge clouds of smoke." Robert turned to him.

"Is the smell of smoke still lingering in the air? No. A fire large enough to take down this house to this state would have taken hours. The wood would still be hot to the touch, but it's not. That could only happen if the fire was started by magic. I mean, I will have them test it, but I'm very positive in my theory."

"Are you sure?" Susan asked.

"Yes, I've seen a couple of these when teenagers start showing off their powers and lose control," he explained.

"But neither Jasmine nor Sasha are magical. There's no way they could start a magical fire; there has to be another explanation." Susan reasoned.

"I don't know what to say." Fred rubbed his neck. "I guess that means someone else started it."

Robert just shook his head. "Before we jump to any conclusion, test the wood to be sure how it started. We need more people here to help find the missing girls," he said.

Fred nodded and went back to work. Robert headed back over to his car and called for reinforcements.

The team gathered back around Robert. The sounds of oncoming traffic resonated through the woods. Six more Enforcer patrol cars and two Fire Control trucks made their way to the house. Within a few minutes, a small crowd had gathered around Robert and Susan.

"Okay everyone, listen up! We have two missing women, Jasmine and Sasha Delant. We have a lot of land to search and no time to waste." Robert said, taking the map from the newly arrived Enforcers and spreading it over the hood of his car. "We are going to break the farm into four quadrants, four people per quadrant. Walk side by side, keep your heads down. Look for any signs of struggle or disturbance. Anything that would show what direction the women might have gone." He waited for them to nod in agreement. "We are right here," he pointed to a spot on the map. "The closest river is about two miles away. They could have gone anywhere between here and there. We have not seen them on any of the main roads, so I am assuming they must have headed into the woods."

"Susan," Robert said, turning everyone's attention to her. "I guess Jasmine knows the land well?"

"Yeah," Susan nodded. "She told me that when she first moved here with her husband Sam, they took walks in the surrounding area. When Sasha got older, they went on camping trips multiple times a year."

"That's good," Robert smiled. "That means they have a better chance of surviving if we are not able to find them tonight."

"But why would they head to the woods? They should have come straight to town," Susan asked.

"It could have been the safer option. If this fire was caused by magic and neither girl had that power, it means someone else started this fire. The woods would have been their best bet for cover and safety." Robert pointed out.

"Now, break up for the grid search."
Robert's voice boomed but was soon
drowned out by the sounds of more sirens
rang through the air. Additional Enforcer
cars came up the driveway followed by
another Fire Control truck.

It seemed as though the entire force was
there, and they were not the only ones
arriving. The townspeople of Blanton and
the local news crew started to approach the
house. Each person trying to see what was
happening at the normally
quiet Delant farm. The arriving Enforcers
and Fire Control officers exited their cars.
They joined Robert and the others who were
still leaning over the map on the hood of his
car.

The news crew and the townspeople
openly gaped at the ruined house.

"Dammit! How did the news find out
about this?" Robert hissed. The last thing he
needed was this getting out before he had
any answers. "We need to push the barriers
back keep them away from the house. I do
not need anyone disturbing the scene. I do
not care what they say – keep everyone
behind the barrier." He motioned to four

Enforcers who had just arrived. They nodded and went to work keeping the curious town back.

"Everyone else gets into groups and get started. We already lost the light, and we cannot afford to waste any more time. I am going to try to appease their curiosity, and with luck, most of them will go home."

Robert turned, and the Enforcers worked on pushing the barrier back. Between the house and the oncoming crowd.

"Everyone listen up!" he yelled as the news crew turned their cameras to him. He ignored the bombarding questions 'What happened?' 'Where are the Delant girls? 'Are they alright?'

"I am only going to say this once. All that I am willing to report at this time is, there was a fire here at the Delant farm. We are currently investigating it as an accident, and that is all. We need everyone to leave and allow us to do our job." Robert made a blatant attempt to avoid Sara Giovanni's eye. She was a reporter who had been a thorn in his side since he became Head Enforcer two years ago. He knew she was ambitious and more than willing to call his bluff, and this situation was no different.

"You expect us to believe this story, Head Enforcer Walsh? How about you tell us what is really going on here? If this was a simple accident, why are there multiple Fire Control trucks? The fire's out. You have dozens of Enforcers doing what I believe is a classic grid search of the farm?" Sara asked. "Also a fire big enough to burn this house down would have created huge clouds of smoke. And I am pretty sure no one in this town saw that today. And here, *right next to the house*, I do not smell any burning embers. The only way *that* happens is if the fire had a magical start. It's obvious something bigger going on here. Why have we not seen the occupants of this house yet? So I ask you again, Head Enforcer Walsh. What is going on?"

Robert took a deep breath, taking a moment to calm his voice. "There is nothing more to report to you. Go home." He walked away knowing he lost this round. Dealing with a nosy reporter was not what he needed to do right now, he needed to focus on what is here and why.

Susan looked around at the structured chaos. *This is not how this day should have gone.* The enforcers were searching the land, some of the more honorable townspeople were stepping up to help, and the news crew started their broadcast.

"Good Evening, I am Sara Giovanni coming to you live from the Small Delant farm. As you can see behind me, we are witnessing the aftermath of what seemed to be a magical fire. A fire that has completely destroyed the Delant home. Though while it has not yet been confirmed by the Enforcers, it's clear to this reporter that Jasmine Delant and her daughter, Sasha, are missing. We will update you as more information becomes available." The camera man signaled that the feed had been cut, and Sara tried to hide her smile as she thought gleefully, *this story will make my career.*

"Susan," a small voice yelled, startling her out of her thoughts and she looked for the owner of the voice. There was Malia Bonta, a plump little lady who was always in everyone's business in town.

"Yes, Ms. Bonta?" Susan answered, politely walking over. Ignoring the fact it was the last thing she wanted to do. She worked hard to never add to Malia's ever-growing list of juicy gossip topics. That woman could talk you to death.

"Susan," she said, grabbing her arm and pulling her close so she could keep her voice down. "You know the Lightworths. Well, they went out of town this morning. I called them later today to make sure they arrived okay, and they told me that their daughter, little Cassie, decided to stay home." Susan sighed as Malia continued to talk about the one thing she truly did not care about at that moment.

"I'm sorry Ms. Bonta, but I do not have the time to talk about this. There are more important things I need to focus on right now." Susan responded, snatching her arm back and trying to get away.

"No!" Malia screeched, resuming her hold. "That is what I am trying to say! She told me that Cassie was going to stay here with Sasha," she finished in a huff. "If Jasmine and Sasha are missing, which we both know they are, so is Cassie – and no one is looking for her!"

"Oh, No!" Susan scanned the crowd for Robert and rushed to him. Someone needed to call Cassie parents before they saw this report on the news.

"Follow her... Follow her..." Sara hissed

to the camera man, pointing him in Susan's direction. "Something big just happened, and I refuse to miss it."

"Enforcer Robert!" Susan yelled to get his attention as she ran towards him. "Cassandra Lightworth was here as well," she cried out once she was close enough to him.

"Are you sure?" The last thing Robert needed was another missing girl, and now he would have to make that phone call he hated.

"Yes. Malia Bonta talked to her parents earlier today. She said Cassie was staying here with the Delants while her parents were away." Susan rushed out.

He hung his head and called over his most trusted Enforcer, George to come over.

"George, you are friends with the Lightworth family, right?"

"Yeah, but they are out of town this week," George replied.

"It turns out that their daughter, Cassie, was here staying with Jasmine and Sasha. I need you to call them and ask if they have heard from Cassie. Get all the information you can before you tell them she is missing."

George hesitated a moment before taking out his phone to call his old friends.

This was one call that Susan did not need to hear. She knew John and Cathy Lightworth, they were great people, and their family had been in this town for years. Cassie was their only child, and everyone knew how close they were as a family.

This news was going to kill them.

Charles, a seasoned Fire Control member, made his way over to Robert after checking the remains of the house. "Robert," he pulled him off to the side. "It seems like Fred's initial assumption was correct. This was a magical fire. On the up side, we did not find any remains in the house, so we know they did escape."

"Did any evidence survive?"

"Not anything we can see. Whoever did this knew what they were doing."

"So we have nothing," Robert surmised.

"Well, I wouldn't go that far." Charles rubbed the back of his neck. "This fire tells us something about the attackers. Controlling fire is a hard thing to do. That is why there are so many Fire Control members. Fire is a living element with a mind of its own. To create a fire from scratch is not hard. But to create enough to consume this entire house, you would definitely need more than one person. If I had to guess I would say at least maybe five or six strong magicals. A magical fire dies fast unless it is constantly fed. But it is draining; since you are using your own energy to fuel it. There had to be at least five to seven people here to finish the job without seriously hurting themselves. The group who did this was powerful."

"Meaning someone did this on purpose." Robert blew out a breath. *"What were these girls mixed up in to land them here?"* he wondered.

Charles nodded. "That's my guess."

"Who would want that?" Susan interjected. "They were the nicest women I have ever met. They don't have any enemies," she stressed.

"How long has Jasmine lived in this area?" Robert turned to Susan, who was barely keeping it together at this point.

"Right before Sasha was born. They moved here after her family died. I think it was a car crash in Iron Grove Cove. She told me they wanted a fresh start."

"George," Robert called, seeing he was

off the phone. Not a good sign in his book. "I need you to head back to the station and call up the Enforcers in Iron Grove Cove. Find out everything you can about Jasmine Delant and get back to me as soon as possible."

"What city?" George asked, and both men turned to Susan for the answer. She mentally ran through every conversation she had with Jasmine. Her eyes were darting back and forth as if she was trying to recall every word.

"I don't know." Susan shook her head. "Every time I asked, she changed the subject or avoided answering. I never thought much about it; I figured she didn't want to talk about it because it was too painful."

"Just start with the major cities and work your way down," Robert ordered. "There has to be a record somewhere. It would have been around 16 years ago," George nodded, headed to the car and back to the base.

Robert turned back to Susan. "I need you to go home," he said, "There is nothing else for you to do here. We are going to continue searching through the night."

"No," Susan argued. "I want to help search. They are like my family; there is no way I could go home not knowing where they are."

"There is nothing left for you to do here. If I find out anything, I promise that you will be the first person I call," Robert said. Susan gave him a small smile and a tiny nod before heading to her car.

Robert gave her a wave as she got in. When she was out of sight, he stepped up onto the patio to address the crowd that continued to gather.

"Can I get your attention?" It took a minute for everyone to quiet down and turn their attention to Robert. "There is nothing left to see here. I understand that most of you know Jasmine and Sasha personally and are worried about their safety. As soon as we have any new information, we will let everyone know. Please go back home to your families." Robert stepped down and went to join the other Enforcers search for the missing girls while the girls drove further from town

Chapter Four

John and Cathy Lightworth were one of
those couples who left no one in doubt about
how they felt about each other. Married for
twenty years and a couple since their teens
years. They often did not need words to
communicate with each other about how
they were feeling. Cathy treasured this
marital shorthand. In all their years together,
this was the first time Cathy wished for once
she could *not* understand the look on her
husband's face. He clenched the phone to
his ear, his face a mixture of pure horror,
fear, and dread. Although Cathy could not
hear the other end of the conversation. She
immediately understood the meaning.
Something was very wrong with Cassandra.

John was in his mid-forties. He often
used his considerable height to intimidate
his daughter's frequent suitors. He ran his
hand through his close-cropped black hair,
closed his tired eyes and dropped his head.
Never in a million years would he expect to

hear the words coming through the phone. Not about his not-so-little angel. *A magical house fire, and now Jasmine and the girls were missing.* He opened his eyes to find his wife looking at him, concern and understanding shining through. His beautiful wife. Her navy blue hair pulled up into one of those messy buns that he loved to pull just to agitate her. Her light blue eyes reflecting only worry and fear. He knew she understood that something was wrong, but didn't know what yet. She knew their daughter was in trouble.

John ended the call with a promise to call back once he had talked to his wife.

"What happened? Was that Jasmine? Did something happen to Cassandra?" Cathy asked as soon as he hung up the phone.

He took a deep breath to collect himself before he answered. "No, that was George. There was a fire at Jasmine's house."

"Are the girls okay?"

"No," he shook his head. "The house is gone, and they are missing - no one knows where they are."

Cathy shrank back. "Our daughter is missing? How? What happened? Was it an accident or a what?

"He..." he blinked back some tears. "He doesn't have the whole story right now, but he said it did not look like an accident. Someone attacked them and burned the house down."

"We need to go. What about the others?" she asked.

"They will understand."

"We leave in ten minutes."

"Make it five," he said as he closed the door behind him.

~

"George," John hugged his friend as he walked into the Enforcer station.

"John, Cathy, I am so sorry." George walked them into Robert's office.

"Please take a seat." Robert shook their hands and walked around to his seat. "I'm sorry we have to meet under these circumstances."

"Have you heard anything new about the girls?" Cathy asked taking a seat.

"No, not yet, there have been no sightings of them or anyone abnormal in the area. I need to know, do you two know if Jasmine had any enemies?"

"Enemies?" John scoffed. "No, she was a farmer, what enemies could she have?" John asked. "Nothing is making sense. We just want to know where our daughter is."

"I want to answer that, I do, but I need to know more about Jasmine."

"What do you want to know?" Cathy asked.

"I need to know about her life."

"Her life? She lived for Sasha and that farm. All she cares about is taking care of her daughter."

"Did she have any money hidden in the house? Did she owe anyone any money?"

"No, nothing like that, Jasmine never owed anyone anything," John answered.

"Are you sure about that?" Robert pushed.

"Yes, she would never put Sasha in any danger. Whoever did this has to have the wrong person."

"It looks as though they were targeted. So there must be a reason. I need you to tell me more." He leaned forward.

"Sir!" George burst into the room. "You need to see this." He turned on the television. He turned it to the national news channel where two anchors sat.

"Last night one of our smaller sister stations reported a horrific attack in their small town. An attack that leads to the disappearance of Jasmine Delant, her daughter Sasha and Sasha's childhood friend Cassandra Lightworth. We now have breaking information regarding Jasmine Delant's history. It seems Jasmine Delant is Jasmine Berlanti. She is a wanted criminal for the attempted murder of a Royal Family Member seventeen years ago."

"And there's my reason." Robert leaned back into his chair. "And there's my headache." He looked out his window to the five men walking on to the floor.

"Who are they?" Cathy turned in her chair.

"Royal Enforcers," George answered.

Robert stood and walked around his desk. "Excuse me for a moment." He nodded to Cathy and John and walked out of his office.

"Hello." Robert outstretched his hand to the men. "I'm Robert Walsh, Head Enforcer here."

The men looked at Robert, ignoring his outstretched hand leaving an awkward pause hanging in the air. Robert got the hint after a moment and dropped his arm.

One of the men stepped forward, asserting himself as the leader. "I am Royal Enforcer Hunter Hopson, and we are here to take over the Delant case." His tone indicated there was no need for pleasantries.

"We just saw the news story. You believe Jasmine Delant is this Jasmine Berlanti?"

"Correct." Hopson nodded.

"How come I've never heard of this attack?" Robert asked.

"We kept it off the public server. The crown didn't want it to get out."

"Then why announce it today?" Robert pushed.

"I do not question their orders I follow them. Just like it is your job to follow orders and your orders now are to hand over this case to my men and me." He left no room for question.

Robert stood his ground and did not comply; he refused to be pushed over in his own house.

"Do we have a problem?" Hunter crossed his arms.

"I would like to see the orders," Robert said.

"I am a Royal Enforcer," Hunter

stressed.

"I understand that," Robert explained. "But I have people in this town who are looking for me to solve this case. No matter who you say Jasmine is, Sasha and Cassie are still cared about by this community. I will not tell them that I just handed the case over without proof or papers."

"I could have you fired." Hunter threatened.

"Show me the orders, and I will give them to you."

Hunter gritted his teeth and adjusted his stance.

"I'll get them for you; there's no need for the orders." Kevin, another enforcer, stood up from his desk, the entire room turned to Kevin, most glaring at him. Kevin Roche was in his forties, with hard steel-black eyes and short graying hair that he liked to attribute to his teenage son. He joined the Enforcers when he turned 18. Even though he was older than Robert and had a few more years on the force, he was passed over for the promotion to Head Enforcer, something he's never gotten over. Ever since then he always tried to undermine Robert any chance he could. This was just another chance.

"Lead the way," Hunter turned to Kevin.

Robert shook his head at Kevin. He knew Kevin was still upset he lost the promotion, but this was the reason why - he had no idea what real loyalty was.

Chapter 5

"This is crazy...right?" Sasha finally spoke up, two hours into their drive to their unknown destination.

"Sasha..." Cassie tried to talk, but Sasha kept going.

"I mean, this is not normal. This doesn't happen to ordinary people." She kept going. "Who were those men, we should stop and go back right?" she slowed the jeep.

"We can't," Cassie reasoned, "Your mom wanted us to head to wherever the coordinates are taking us."

"I know but Cassie." She pulled the jeep to a stop and turned it off. "We should go to the enforcers."

"Your mom said-"

"They took my mom!" Sasha screamed into the darkness. "Running away isn't helping her, we need to go back, we need to help her." Sasha cried, tears freely falling down her face. "They took her, and they destroyed our house!"

"She gave herself up to protect you!" Cassie argued. "She said don't trust anyone until we get to the safe point. We're not there yet." She took a breath. "What if we go back there and they're waiting for you...for us... we could walk right into a trap."

Sasha clenched her eyes and scrubbed her face repeatedly with her hands, angrily wiping away her falling tears. "She's all I have Cassie," she cried.

"She wanted you to get away, I think... I believe it would be best if we go where she wanted. You never know who we are meeting. They could be people in place to help us save her."

Sasha let out a dark laugh. "Do you think that, really?"

"I'm hoping," Cassie said.

Sasha dropped her head to the steering wheel. "I just want some answers."

"I know." Cassie rubbed her back, and Sasha cried. "How about you let me take over driving? You should get some rest."

"Like I could sleep right now..." Sasha shook her head.

"Then, read the journal." Cassie plucked it from Sasha's bag and handed it over. "Maybe you can start to get some of those answers."

"Fine." She shrugged and hopped out of the jeep as Cassie slid over to the driver seat. Sasha did a quick jog around the car and hopped back in. Cassie started the jeep back up and continued down the dark road.

They drove in silence for a few minutes until Cassie turned on the radio. "Let's listen to some tunes," she said, flipping through the channels trying to find a good one.

"Wait! Go back!" Sasha grabbed the dial and turned the knob. "I think I heard something." She turned the dial back a few stations and turned up the volume.

"It's crazy!" The voice said. "That small little town has to face an attack like that, and from the reports, Jasmine and her daughter Sasha are missing,"

"Let's not forget Sasha's friend Cassie was also there during the attack." Another voice came through.

"The story made it to the news already." Cassie turned it down.

"That's quick!" Sasha commented.

"It's only been like," she glanced at the clock. "A couple of hours since the attack, how is it on the news?"

"At least it means someone will start looking into what happened to us," Cassie said, keeping her eyes on the road. Sasha knew Cassie never liked to drive at night and this back road they were on wasn't the best.

"Looking for us as we drive away..." Sasha pointed out.

"Yes," Cassie rolled her eyes. "Looking for what happened. They could find out who is behind the attack."

Sasha leaned back against the headrest trying to collect her thoughts. "I know I sound like a broken record, but I just don't understand. Who would do this?"

Cassie shrugged her shoulders; she had no answer to give her.

~

Sasha gripped the steering wheel tighter glancing every few seconds in her rear view mirror. For the last thirty minutes of their drive, they were being followed, or at least she thought they were. She had taken over from Cassie once the sun started to rise a few hours ago and now Cassie was getting some much-needed rest.

However, for the last thiry minutes, that truck had been there. At first, she didn't give it a second thought. She knew there was a chance they would run into other cars on the drive but they passed many exits, and the truck never left its spot behind them.

She didn't want to wake up Cassie just in case she was over reacting, but they would need to stop to fuel up soon. She didn't want to risk it if they were indeed being followed.

She took another glance in the mirror. The truck was getting closer. Sasha slowed down and rolled down the window and stuck out her hand motioning for them to pass her.

The truck sped up, and Sasha turned her head from the window to block their view of her face as they sped past her.

She let out a breath once they passed and kept going down the road and took the exit up a head. They were not following them.

She drove another 20 miles to make sure the truck did not come back on the road and pulled over.

"Cassie wake up." She shook her

gently.

"What," Cassie rubbed her eyes and looked at the clock. "It's not the time to change seats."

"I know," Sasha unbuckled her seatbelt. "We are about to run out of gas; I need you to watch out while I fill up the tank." She walked around to the back of the jeep and pulled out the gas can.

Cassie sat up and kept a look out while Sasha filled the tank.

"We shouldn't need to stop for a bit after this," Sasha said. "If you need to go, now would be the time to do it." She pulled the gas can out of the back and placed the empty canister back in the jeep.

"I think I will." Cassie hopped out the truck and stretched her body and walked a few feet into the woods while Sasha stood guard.

In a few minutes, Cassie came back, and Sasha switched with her. In five minutes they were back on the road, and Cassie was falling back asleep.

Sasha kept her eyes peeled and drove off. She had another two hours before they were going to switch.

Chapter Six

Sasha stared out the window as the green scenery sped passed her. It was Cassie's turn to drive again. So far they have been driving for a day and a half, switching every four hours. They only stopped to refuel the truck. With what they had left in the tank, it seemed they only had just enough to get to wherever they were going.

Sasha was amazed by how many back roads there were. Never knew how many back roads there were. During the entire drive not once did they ever set foot on a major highway. They only passed a few cars. In their current direction, they were able to narrow down the possibilities of their destination. There were headed somewhere in the providence of Ramshire.

She read through the journal a couple of times for more answers, but nothing was truly making sense. At least not without the right context. On top of that, there were so many blank pages scattered throughout the book. What she focused on most, was the list of simple spells that her mother said she would most likely need to stay safe. She read and re-read that section over and over.

For as long as she could remember, she felt as if there was a part of her that was missing. Now for the first time in forever, she felt whole.

She reached up for the necklace that was no longer there. She still couldn't believe what Cassie said.

Cassie suggested it was most likely a modified wizard necklace. Generally, they were used to bind the powers of wizards who broke the law, and for years her parents used it to keep her powers from her.

"So who do you think we are going to meet?" Cassie asked bringing Sasha out of her thoughts.

Sasha shrugged. "Same answer as last time, I have no idea."

"And there is nothing in her journal at all about it?"

"Again No," Sasha leaned back in her chair.

Cassie opened her mouth, but Sasha turned the radio back on and started to flip through the stations. "Maybe there is another story about us."

"It's only been like a day. Do you think they found anything new?"

"Who knows, but I hope so." She turned until she found a news station. They waited, listening to the weather report for a few minutes until the news story started.

"We have more information about the attack on the Delant farm. We have received reports that Jasmine Delant was the target of this attack. According to reports from Royal Enforcers, Jasmine Delant is Jasmine Berlanti. She is wanted for crimes against the crown. The Royal Enforcers believe someone from her unsavory past has now come after her. They do not think Sasha is involved in her mother's actions. They believe she and Cassie are innocent bystanders in this horrible situation."

"What?" Sasha turned down the radio. "No, that can't be true," she shook her head. "My mom is not some criminal. What is happening to my life?"

"Sasha..."

"I don't want to talk right now!" She closed her eyes and turned to face the window.

"Ok," Cassie whispered focusing on the

road.

"I'm sorry you got roped into this," she whispered after a bit. "You could have gone back to town. You didn't have to come."

"I would never let you go through this alone. We have no idea who attacked us. It might not be safe for me to go back either. It is safer for both of us to stay together."

"Still thank you," Sasha said as she leaned back in her chair and covered her eyes.

Cassie drummed her fingers along the top steering wheel and glanced over at Sasha. She knew her friend needed her now more than ever. She couldn't understand why Jasmine kept Sasha's powers from her. Sasha was very powerful; Cassie never saw anyone Sasha's age stop a fire that strong by accident. Cassie recalled how she could see the magic bouncing off Sasha skin - it was raw and unstable, but it was strong.

She shook her head and refocused on the road. The first thing she needed to worry about was where they were going. They had only a few more hours left and she just hoped where ever they ended up was safe...and had a shower. Two full days of being in a car under the hot sun equal two very sweaty teen girls.

She also wanted a real meal, a hot meal. The granola and dried fruit kept them from hunger, but it was not as satisfying as they hoped. She focused on the mountains that were in the far off distance. According to the GPS, once they crossed over those mountains, they were just about there. She just needed to focus on the drive.

~

"Sasha," Cassie gently shook her. "Wake up; we are here."

"Hmm," Sasha turned over in her seat.

"Get up; we are here. Well…wherever here is." She looked around at the dense forest.

Sasha sat up rubbed the sleep out of her eyes and looked around. "We are in the middle of a forest, are you sure?"

"Yeah. I checked and double checked. All I know is we are somewhere outside the City of Widener."

"Widener, that's all the way on the edge of Ramshire."

"Yeah, we drove down the coast for a bit, quite a beautiful view."

"Yet we are still in the middle of the forest."

"Yeah, according to the GPS," she lifted it to recheck the route. "We have to hike from this point. I pulled the car in as deep as I could, but it still looks like we are going to walk from here."

"How long of a hike?" Sasha grabbed her bag from the back seat and hopped out of the jeep.

Cassie grabbed her bag, the GPS unit, and followed Sasha out of the jeep. "Looks like just over an hour, want to carry me?" she gave Sasha her best puppy dog eyes.

"Not on your life." Sasha snorted. "You can put those away. I'm immune to your puppy dog look. They only work on the boys in our class."

"One day it will work on you." Cassie laughed.

"Not any day soon." She bumped shoulders. "Ugh... why couldn't she just spell out where we are going? Why all the secrets?"

"I can answer that." A soft voice answered from behind them, causing the girls to whip around. Sasha faulted.

"Mom?" she said in disbelief of the women standing in front of her.

The woman shook her head. "No, I'm

sorry I am not your mother. My name is Wendy, and I am your mother's twin sister. I'm your Aunt."

Chapter Seven

Robert rubbed the back of his neck as he looked out to his enforcers. He sighed and glanced back at the reports on his desk. Well, his copy at least. The Royal Enforcers were getting first dibs on all information going in and out of this office. The report agreed with Charles and Fred's earlier theory. There were multiple attackers, and this was a magical fire. With the new information about Jasmine, the attack was now making sense. The major question now was: Were the women even missing or were they kidnapped? He needed to find more information, hopefully before Hudson and his men did.

"George," Robert called, placing the reports on the table. If he didn't get the information before Hudson, he knew he would never get the whole story.

"Yes sir," George answered, walking into the office a few moments later.

"Let's go on a lunch break." Robert stood and grabbed his coat.

"Sir?" George questioned.

"I need answers before the Royal Enforcers get them. Something about this story of Jasmine is not sitting right with me."

"So where should we go for lunch?" George asked again.

"I'm thinking some place with a nice view," he headed out of the office, George right behind them.

As they pulled up to the house, George got out of the car and stared at the remains. "So what are you expecting to find during our lunch break?."

"Anything that will lead us to the truth of what happened here." Robert walked up the steps and into what remained of the house.

"What about the Royal Enforcers?"

"I have been an Enforcer for a long time. Never have I heard of keeping an attempt on the Royal Family lives under wraps. I am not sure of what is going on, but they are hiding something, I am just not sure what it is."

"What are you expecting to find today that we haven't already?" George started to look around the room.

"When we first searched we had the mindset that the girls were victims with nothing to hide. Today we know different. Today we know that Jasmine is a wanted criminal. That means she had something to hide. We are looking for clues to where she could have hidden any information."

"The house is gone, what do you expect to find in all this rubble?" George watched Robert walk around, moving things with the toe of his shoe.

"I expect to find something like this," Robert said, crouching down and moving some burned debris out of his way.

"What is it?" George moved in for a closer look.

Robert made a waving motion with his hand and moved some of the heavier debris out of the way. "I stepped on a loose floor board." He pulled it up. "She had a trap door," he stared down the opening.

"How did they miss this?" George asked in mild surprise.

"No one was looking for a trap door; they were looking for bodies," Robert said.

"Should I call for others?" George asked, reaching for his phone.

"No, I want to see what is down here first. Once we call this in, Hunter and his men will be all over this. If we tell them, we will never get another chance to see whatever she was hiding." He climbed down the stairs, and the darkness greeted him once he touched the bottom. He ran his hand along the wall, looking for a light switch, and flicked it on once he found it. "It looks like they came down here," Robert said as the destroyed room greeted him.

"Looks like whoever was after them found this room as well," George said as he came down the steps.

"Let's hope they got away first." Robert pointed to the gaping hole in the wall.

"My guess is they were caught," George said. "That would explain the room. It looks like a fight took place."

"By the look of the opening, I think someone got away first." Robert watched his steps making sure not to ruin the scene. "The door is blown open. If you have a hidden door, you have a way to open it. I think they got the door opened and closed it behind them before whoever attacked them got down here."

"And they blew the door." George

finished. "I wonder how far this tunnel goes?" he looked down the opening.

Robert created several light balls and sent them down the tunnel. The men watched as the lights floated down the dark tunnel. They floated further and further away until they were specks of light in the distant.

"You can barely see them."

"Let's take a look." Robert stepped through the opening with George after him. Robert made a few more balls of light and let them float around them.

"This must have taken years," George commented running his hand along the dirt wall. "It feels dry; it's been exposed to air for a while."

"How was she able to keep this a secret?" Robert said. "You can't build this without someone noticing. All this dirt was displaced it had to go somewhere."

"They live next to the woods, and they have a farm. It would be easy to move it around with no one the wiser."

Robert had to agree with that line of thought.

"She has been planning this for years," Robert stated once they reached the end of the tunnel.

"Three more tunnels?" George gasped.

"One of them looks caved in. Time to call this in. We can't search them all ourselves, who knows how many more tunnels are at the end of each of these." Robert shook his head.

"Hunter is going to take over," George stated.

"I know," Robert sighed and pulled the light balls back in. "But there is nothing I can do about that. There is no way I can keep this off the record." Robert turned and headed back to the basement.

"Hunter is a douche bag." George groaned.

"Yes, but he has jurisdiction over this case," Robert said.

Once they made it out of the tunnel, Robert pulled out his phone to make a call that every cell in his body knew was wrong. "Hunter, it's Robert, I am out at the Delant farm, and I believe I found how she escaped." He paused letting Hunter speak. "Yes, I understand this case is your case which is why I am calling to let you know I found something. I will see you out here shortly." He hung up the phone.

"Where do you want to wait?" George asked.

"Upstairs, I'm not in the mood to get kicked out of my crime scene." Robert headed up the stairs.

They were leaning on their car when they saw the Royal Enforcer cars pull up, Kevin with them of course.

"What did you find?" Hunter cut straight to the point.

"I can show you," Robert pushed off his car.

"No need, just point me in the right direction." Hunter stopped him.

Robert swallowed his retort as he caught the smug look on Kevin's face. "There is a trap door that leads to a basement that's not on any of our blueprints. There's a tunnel down there."

"A tunnel?" Hunter brows furrowed. "How far?"

"At least a mile," George cut in. "Then there were three more tunnels."

"Good work." Hunter nodded. "My men and I can take over from here."

"Good luck."

Robert and George watched from inside the car as the men descended onto the crime scene.

"We need to go see Susan," Robert said as he started his car and headed down the long driveway.

"Why?"

"There is no way she could have been friends with Jasmine for this long and not known about her secret life. Hunter and his crew will be busy down there for a while. It gives us plenty of time to learn a bit more."

Chapter Eight

"My mom has a sister? You're my aunt?" Sasha took a step back. The woman in front of her was her mother's twin in every way. Except where her mother had brown hair and brown eyes, this woman had black hair and black eyes.

"Yes," Wendy nodded. "These are my sons." She pointed to the twin boys flanking her. They were both tall at least six feet each, with jet black hair, black eyes, and a slightly darker complexion. Their differences came with their physical makeup. One twin was a bit more muscular than the other. He had his hair cut short to his head while his twin was on the lankier side with long hair and glasses. "This is Danny," the muscular twin nodded his head, "...and Devin," the thinner twin nodded his head.

"Hey." Sasha waved before lowering her arm when they didn't wave back. "Well I guess you know who I am, but this is my friend Cassie, she was there when this all happened," she explained. "But wait, why are you waiting on us? How did you know we would be here?"

"The GPS you used to get here is connected to my computer. Once it was activated and you began your journey here, it alerted me. It was a fail-safe Jasmine, and I implanted just in case one of us was found." Wendy answered.

"Where are we exactly?" Cassie looked around the forest.

"About an hour away from our home. It will be getting dark soon; we should get going." Wendy walked past the two girls and headed deeper into the woods.

"Wait!" Sasha followed. "I have a ton of questions. Can you tell us why we needed to come here in the first place?"

"No," Wendy called over her shoulder.

"Why?" Cassie countered.

"Because we are too exposed out here. I will tell you once we are in the safety of my home." She called over her shoulder. "So the faster you move, the faster you get your answers."

"She cannot be serious," Sasha whispered to Cassie.

"She is, so go faster." Danny passed them and followed his mother with Devin bringing up the rear.

Sasha and Cassie shared a look but quietly followed Sasha's new family to their safe point.

~

"We are here," Wendy called as they reached the bottom of a cliff.

"Please tell me you do not expect us to climb this." Cassie looked up the side of the cliff dropping her bag to the ground. "We just came off the worse road trip ever with little to no sleep, then that awful hike."

"No, but if you want to try, I'll be happy to watch." Danny came up beside her. "I've done it a couple of times, I'll be glad to give you pointers." he winked.

Cassie rolled her eyes. "I see which twin you are." She grumbled.

"The entrance is over here." Wendy walked over to a boulder and placed her hand on it. Her hand glowed a bright green and an opening formed near them. "Through here." she motioned with her head.

"What is with your family and secret openings?" Cassie whispered picking her bag up and following Sasha into the doorway. "Not what I was expecting," she said as she took in the room.

"Yes, I figured since we lived in a cliff I should make an effort to make it more welcoming and less as we lived in a cave." Wendy closed the door.

"It's nice," Sasha added. "But now that we are here do you mind telling us what happened at my home and why we need to be here. Then answer the other million questions I'm waiting to ask."

"Follow me; you can leave your bags here, Danny and Devin will take them to your room." She headed down the hall.

They gratefully dropped their bags on the floor and followed Wendy. They walked down the hall and down the stairwell into her office.

"I told Jasmine that keeping you in the dark was a mistake," she started. "I told her you needed to know our family history from the beginning. But she feared that you would follow in her footsteps if you did." Wendy took a seat behind her desk, and Sasha and Cassie sat across from her. "What do you girls know about Gabriella Botticelli, the daughter of King Francis Botticelli?" she asked.

Sasha thought for a moment trying to remember history class. "She umm… she killed her father, King Francis. He was going to take the crown from her and give it to her younger brother. She escaped before anyone could find her, but she was later found and killed. Almost ten years later. What does that have to do with us?"

"Before she was found, she married the guard who helped her escape, and they had a child," Wendy explained. "Her daughter is my grandmother, Jasmine's grandmother."

"Wait…" Sasha felt all the air exit her body. "Are you saying what I think you are?" Wendy nodded. "No," Sasha denied. "I refuse to believe we are related to that traitor, no."

"She was not a traitor, she was framed," Wendy explained.

"Framed?" Cassie asked. "By who?"

"Her stepmother. Queen Victoria was behind it."

"And why would she do that?" Sasha asked in utter disbelief.

"When the Botticelli's fought for the throne all those years ago, during the forming of our country, they beat the opposing family that was fighting for power

90

as well - the Vermeil's."

"But in school, we learned they were all killed during the war. The last of them committed suicide; they burned their home down. They mailed a note to a friend saying they didn't want to live under the rule of their most hated enemies." Cassie interrupted.

"That was the world's understanding, but instead they went into hiding. No one knew it at the time. They hid and took their time until they were in enough power to be in the presence of the King through a false name." she explained.

"You know you are talking about years of planning right. Like over three hundred years' worth." Sasha said. "Who could hold a grudge for that long?"

"I understand that, but it doesn't mean that they didn't go underground and they worked on their plan. For generations, they planned to get back what they thought was theirs. They had a member of their family join the castle and poison the Queen, Gabriella's mother. When she died, Victoria had her opening to be with the King."

"Then she kills him?" Sasha asked.

"Yes," Wendy nodded. "She gave birth

to her lover's child, unbeknownst to the King of course. Once he accepted the child as his and the world accepted it, he was no longer needed. Once she had a male heir, the king and his daughter were no longer of any use. She killed him and framed Gabriella for it. Sadly once Gabriella ran, she sealed her fate as guilty."

"How was no one able to prove her innocence, she should have been able to prove it. She was the princess!" Sasha stated.

"Yeah, you would think that, but the facts were not on her side. At the time people were pushing for the King to announce his son as his heir, not Gabriella. The night before his death, they had a loud argument, one overheard by many in the castle."

"But the crown goes to the first born," Cassie said.

"And up until that point all the firstborns had been male, they wanted it to continue. They said the King was leaning towards agreeing with them. The world would know she had the motive to kill her father to keep the crown. So once the guard found the King murdered they ran to her room to protect her."

"How do you know all of this?" Cassie asked.

"There were a few guards that remained loyal to Gabriella. After she had escaped, they worked to find the clues that could clear her. They were able to find this but not enough to prove she was innocent. Before she was captured, she wrote it all down so we would always know the truth."

"Why not go to the press about it, get her side of the story out, why not do that now?"

Wendy shook her head. "Jasmine and I asked that very same question once our parents told us."

"Why tell you if they have no plan for fixing it?" Sasha asked.

"So we would never forget the truth. We were safe; the crown never knew we existed, we were able to lead normal lives."

"So how did they find us now?" Sasha asked. "And if we could have normal lives why do you live off the grid in a mountain, and why did my mom lie to me. Also, why are they calling her a criminal?" she pushed further.

"I'm not sure how, but a few years ago before you were born, they found us. I don't know how but they did. They killed my parents and my aunt and her husband. The only reason Jasmine and I are alive is because we were not home."

"Why not stay together?" Cassie asked.

"Jasmine was traveling when it happened; we knew it wasn't safe for her to journey to where I was so we agreed to split up. We found a way to keep in contact, but we had to assume new identities. We hoped they wouldn't find us, but clearly, I was wrong."

"So what do we do now?" Sasha asked.

"Now we lay low. No one knows where my sons or I live. There will be no going into town anymore. We need to wait it out until the search dies down."

"What about me?" Cassie asked. "I need to get back to my parents; they must be worried sick about me by now. They need to know I am ok."

"I will be honest with you Cassie, right now I have no idea what to do about you. You were never in the plan to be here. That being said, I promise you I will find a way to get you home. But right now I need to make sure it will not endanger the rest of us. As well as make sure you will not become a target once you are home." Wendy explained.

"Oh," Cassie nodded. "How long do you think it will take?"

"Probably a couple of weeks I need to wait to see how they will play this out. But it does look good that they are reporting you two are innocent bystanders. In the public eye, you will have their sympathy."

"I understand." She swallowed, her stomach suddenly feeling heavy.

"If I can push it up, I will, but I will not risk anyone's safety right now."

"What about my mom, how do we save her?" Sasha asked. "She gave herself up so we could get away."

Wendy hesitated. "Sasha," she started slowly. "We can't save her."

"But she's your sister," Sasha argued. "My Mom."

"It would be a death sentence to go after her. We agreed years ago that if either one of us were taken the other would protect her family."

"So you would let each other die?"

"Sasha there is no winning against them. Our best chance of surviving is laying low for a few years."

"No!" Sasha shook her head. "You cannot possibly expect me to accept that. I will not leave my mother to die."

"Sasha," Wendy leaned forward in her seat. "You need to understand something. You were sent here to live, not to help save her."

Chapter Nine

Robert pulled into Susan's driveway and cut the engine. They exited the car and headed up to her front door and knocked. They had waited for a few quiet seconds before Robert knocked again. "Susan, it's Enforcers Robert and George. We have a few more questions to ask you." He called through the door giving it a hard knock.

"Maybe she's not here?" George asked, peeking through the window but the blinds were pulled shut. "She might be at work…"

"No," Robert shook his head. "Something is not right." He grasped the door handle, and his hand glowed before the handle opened with a slight click.

"What are you doing?" George asked, "We cannot break into her house. That's for emergencies only."

"This is an emergency," Robert replied, entering the home and paused taking in the scene. "This is why she didn't come to the door." Robert glanced down at her motionless body.

Susan laid dead at their feet. Only a few feet from the door, her lifeless eyes staring up at the ceiling, her arm stretched out. Her clothes were bloodied and torn, and bruises covered what skin they could see.

She had ripped tape around her ankles and wrist and, from what they could see, a piece of tape hanging from her mouth. Around her neck was a magical blocking necklace.

"Damn," George muttered under his breath. By the way, her body was laid out; it looked like she was trying to escape. She was almost at the door, almost free from whoever attacked her.

"Call it in," Robert ordered and stepped around her body. "And be careful where you step. I'm going to clear upstairs."

George reached for his phone, called in the murder, and started to clear his current level. In his initial overlook, it looked like she put up a fight before they overpowered her. The pictures hanging on the wall were shattered. Her furniture destroyed. Papers were strewn all over the floor. There were dents in the wall, and he hoped Susan's body wasn't what made them.

Every room on the first level matched that of the living room. It seemed the fight went all over the house.

"George!" Robert called as he descended the stairs.

"In the kitchen!" George answered.

"It looks like whoever did this was looking for something. Upstairs is ransacked."

"This has to be connected to who attacked Jasmine. Susan was her closest friend. If Jasmine got away, they might have thought Susan would know where she might go."

"Unfortunately, I think you are correct." Robert agreed. "Did you check her garage?"

"Not yet, it was my next stop."

Robert walked out the side door and into her garage. Like the rest of the house, everything was over thrown. He watched his steps, and he worked around the room looking for anything that might be out of place.

"Find anything?" George joined him.

"I can't tell if they found whatever they were looking for."

"What is this?" George pushed the over turned workbench to the side.

"George what are you doing. We need to preserve the scene."

"There is a trap door under here." He pulled at the latch. The door was a bit heavier than the one they encountered at Jasmine's house.

"Two women in my town both hiding secret basements," Robert muttered walking down the steps after George. It was smaller than Jasmine's. This room was just big enough to hold George and himself and a small desk with a laptop on it and a chair.

"Pretty tight in here," George commented taking in the small space. "I wonder why she kept her computer down here."

"I saw a broken one in her office upstairs, this is an extra one," Robert answered. "We need to get Kaitlin on this; she is a wiz on these things." He sent out a quick message from his phone. Kaitlin Miller made history as the first female non-magical to join the town of Blanton Enforcer team. She was a petite woman in her early twenties who at first received a lot of push back from the mostly male, mostly older, all magical team. Robert had just been promoted to captain, and she was one of his first hires. He offered to help her out, but she wanted no part of it. She was strong and pushed back in her way. What she lacked in magical abilities she made up for technical skills. Put her on a computer and she could and would if provoked or ordered, use her abilities to do damage. If there was anyone in the world, who could find something on this computer it was her.

"You are only in your forties, you are not allowed to call laptops 'these things'," George shook his head.

"Enforcer George?" A voice called from above them.

"Coming up!" George answered maneuvering around Robert and headed up the short steps. Robert took one last look around the small space and followed George up the steps.

It did not take long before the neighborhood realized something was up. More Enforcers were pulling up by the minute, along with the crime scene techs. As they wheeled Susan's body down the steps and into the corner's van the size of the onlookers grew to twice the size of what was at Jasmine's house. Robert peeked out the window and saw the bane of his existence. Sara was out there setting up her camera getting ready to go live with this new story.

"Please tell me someone found prints or anything that will lead to whoever did this. I will even take a hand written confession." He called to his men.

Some of the men around the room let out a small laugh. Robert walked back into the garage where Kaitlin was. She was busy trying to figure out why Susan had a hidden laptop.

"Were you able to find anything yet?" he leaned against the doorway.

"I think I figured out why she had this extra laptop." She sat it down on the table. "She was using this laptop to spy on Jasmine."

"On Jasmine are you sure, not for Jasmine?" Robert asked. "I thought they were friends?"

"Yeah, she was sending weekly reports of Jasmine's life to some person. I tried to track some of the emails, but she covered her tracks well. I can't figure out who she was sending these emails to yet, but with some time I should be able. What I do have is the last report that she was working on, she wasn't done yet."

"Head back to the station and continue to work on the problem and print out the report you do have and send it to me."

"No problem," Kaitlin stood and started to gather her equipment.

"Oh, and Kaitlin," Robert pulled her to the side. "Do whatever you can as fast as you can, I want as much as you can get to me before Hunter gets wise of this situation."

"Sure thing." She closed the laptop and headed out the garage door into the growing mob scene on Susan Comesto's front lawn.

Robert watched Kaitlin drive off from the window and groaned when he saw Hunter's car pull up. He had hoped the tunnel would keep them busy for longer than a couple of hours.

Chapter Ten

Sasha stared at the ceiling and concluded sleep was not coming tonight. It was her first night in Wendy's home, and her restlessness was nothing new - she always had issues sleeping in a new place. A snore from Cassie told her she was the only one who was having a problem with their sleeping arrangements. She rolled herself over into a sitting position and walked over to the door and left. She walked silently down to the hall to the small living room.

Against the wall was a built-in bookshelf filled with volumes of books, some looking older than she was. She ran her finger down the spines as she read the titles. She hesitated against the small leather journal with Gabriela's name embossed in beautiful script. She plucked the journal off the shelf and settled on the couch and started to read.

Hello,

I'm not quite sure how to write this, or where to begin. I am writing this for one reason only. The truth…I know I will never make people believe my story, but I want you, my family, to know what happened. I was twelve when my life changed.

I should have noticed something was amiss when my mother passed but grief blinded me to the truth. My mother was murdered; they disguised it as a common cold. They took her from my father and me. The royal doctor died a month earlier, a hunting accident, but now I am sure they killed him too.

I was always uncomfortable around the new doctor. She seemed to get worse after a visit with him. At the time we thought that her condition worsened due to her illness, But now I know he was making her worse. He was killing my mother in front of my father and me, and we were none the wiser.

The day of her funeral broke me. I remember staring out the window to the gardens, my mother's favorite spot in the castle. Now to be my mother's final resting place. My personal guard John, he used to call me 'little miss,' told me not to be sad. Ever the proper child I was, I told him 'I am sad, so sad I will act.' I know he was only looking out for me, but that day I couldn't see past my grief.

My father pulled me into his office before the ceremony to have a private word with me. He asked me to remain strong ... to uphold the family image. I knew his heart ached much more than mine, but he wanted us to stay strong for our people. They would always look to us for strength. He did allow me my time to grieve once I was safely tucked away from the prying eyes of the world.

It was hard, to keep strong, but I knew I could do this for my mother and my people. I can still feel the hug he gave me, the last hug before it all changed. My grandparents were there. They were allowed to weep publicly for their fallen child. I remember walking the flower covered path to my seat. The garden full of life, except the one I wanted most.

I blocked out most of the funeral; I didn't want my last memory of my mother to be filled with the words of others. I did not want their memories of her. I wanted to keep my memories, the happy times, never that day, never. The kingdom mourned their Queen, a title, which can be replaced. I mourned my mother ... a role no one could ever fill.

The receiving line was where I first saw her. I will give her this; she knew not to be the first in line. She waited until she was one of the last women to pass my father's eye. She was beautiful. Her beauty masked the evil that stewed inside of her.

Victoria.

She claimed to be a former friend of my mother. That was a lie. I knew about all my mother's friends and not once had she ever mentioned her. She lied, but I had no proof. She smiled her way into my father's life, and there was nothing I could do to stop her.

It happened so fast...I never expected it to happen that quickly. Barely two years passed since my mother's death, and my father was remarrying. I laughed at the thought. My father wanted to be happy, and I could see he was just trying to mask the pain I knew him to be in. He loved my mother, but he did not want to be alone.

I'm not a horrible daughter who never wanted her father to move on. It was just that Victoria was not the right woman. She was not the kind of woman my father should marry.

I tried to stop it; I argued that he was

trying to replace my mother. Not the best choice of words. He was angry at me for even suggesting he could love anyone like he loved my mother. She was his light in a dark tunnel, his other half. I asked then why ever be with anyone else. He only told me everything would be ok. I was a child, powerless to stop the pain I knew this woman was going to cause.

She requested I be in the room as she readied. I knew it was only to show off that she won. She knew I didn't like her or trust her. I watched as they dressed her in her wedding dress. If you could call it that...

I have never seen anything tackier, and when she walked down the aisle, I saw the minor look of shock on my father's face. She would never hold a candle to the class and elegance my mother always exuded.

My grandparents were happy that my father was moving on, that my mother would have wanted it. It seemed like I was the only one who saw this woman for what she was.

I played my part well during the ceremony. I clapped and cheered at all the right moments but inside I was dying. Dying because Victoria was trying to destroy my family...

"Sasha?"

Her head shot up, and she clapped the book shut turning to face the intruding voice.

"Devin?" she asked.

"What are you doing up?" he came further into the room.

"Oh umm," she held up the journal shaking it slightly. "I couldn't sleep so I decided to read a bit. Is that ok?"

"Yeah, that's fine." He yawned dropping in the seat next to hers.

"What are you doing up?" she asked.

"I always wake up around this time and do a walkthrough of the house."

"Why?"

"I've always done it." He shrugged and plucked the journal out of her hands. "This is good," he commented.

"You've read it?" Sasha asked.

"I've read them all." He pointed to the wall. "I do live here." He laughed.

"This is true." She laughed before calming herself down. "Can I ask you a serious question?"

"Shoot." He leaned back.

"How have you guys survived? Here I mean."

"Because we have to, though I do hate it." Devin shrugged. "We live isolated from the world. We go into town only twice a month for supplies. I've always wanted to have a normal life. To live in an ordinary town and go to school. But I guess what happened at your house is proof that this needed to be done. But this isn't a way to live."

"Yeah, but you knew the truth. My mom kept this all from me. My head feels like it's spinning. And to know that I can't save her," she cleared her throat.

"I'm sorry Sasha," Devin said.

"It's not your fault." Sasha sighed. "This situation just sucks. I just want to wake up and have this all to be a nightmare. How do you deal with it?"

"It's all I've ever known. I'll help you get used to it."

"I'm not sure I will ever be used to it."

"It could take a few years, but you will get there."

"Thanks," she smiled feeling her eyes get a bit heavier. "I think I'm going to try and get some sleep. Your Mom said she would train me in the morning." She stood.

"Good night," he handed her the journal.

"Night," she smiled and left the room. Sasha climbed back into bed and placed the journal on her night table. She dropped her head to the pillow and closed her eyes.

Chapter Eleven

"Sasha, your training might be a bit tricky." Wendy opened the door to what Sasha could only call a rubber room.

"Why?"

"Well for starters, most children grow with their powers. Your powers feed off your energy. As you grow you become stronger and are more able to sustain yourself when you use them. But the issue I see with you is, since your mother kept yours locked from you, you did not grow with them."

"Meaning?" Sasha prompted.

"Meaning your ability to handle your powers might be low."

"It's just a might be, though?"

"Could be, let's see what you can handle. What have you done so far?"

Sasha shrugged. "Stopping the flame during the fire, and when the men who attacked us tried to get in the house, I attacked them. I'm not sure what I did.

Cassie used her powers through me to exit the tunnel."

"How did you feel after?"

"I'm not sure," she shrugged. "It all felt like a complete rush. I wasn't focused on my energy level."

"Did you sleep as soon as you got in the truck?"

"No," she shook her head, "Cassie said she thought I was powerful when she closed the tunnel door, but we never talked about it."

Wendy nodded and walked to the side of the room and opened the small trunk and pulled out a small rubber ball. "Just to be on the safe side we will start with the basics." She held out her hand with the ball. "Do you know how to move it?"

"No, like I said when I used my powers, it was if they were working on their own." Sasha shook her head.

"You need to think of your powers as an extension of yourself. Think of them as extra hands; you want the ball to move. So move it."

"Ok…" Sasha nodded taking a breath.

"Just think about what you want to be done," Wendy instructed.

Sasha closed her eyes and thought of all the times she saw Cassie use her powers. All the times she witnessed anyone using their powers. She held out her hand like she saw Cassie do a million times and called the ball to her.

Her hand glowed bright, and the ball flew from Wendy's hand. It slammed into the wall behind Sasha with a loud slap before bouncing around the room. The sound echoed in the small room.

"Ok," Wendy brought the ball back to her hand. "How about we try that again but softer, and remember this room is part of my home."

"That was soft...I think??" Sasha scratched the back of her head.

"Ok, in that case, extra soft." Wendy retorted.

Sasha nodded and waved her hand again. The ball flew from Wendy's palm and hit Sasha's forearm with a hard slap.

"Ouch!" she yelped as the ball fell to the ground. She rubbed her arm where a small red mark was currently forming. She was surprised it didn't break the skin.

"That was soft-ish," Wendy brought the ball back to her hand. "Still too hard but we can work on control later. I am happy to see you can use your powers with ease." Wendy smiled. "Let's try something different. This time I am going to send the ball towards you, and I want you to stop it. Make a shield."

Sasha shrugged. "How do I do that?"

"Think of a glass wall protecting you. It needs to be thick and vigorous."

"Got it!" Sasha nodded and focused on a wall protecting her when she felt like she had one she nodded to Wendy.

Wendy allowed the ball to float in front of her for a moment then sent it flying towards Sasha. Off instinct, Sasha's hands shot up to protect her face from impact.

"Stop!" Wendy instructed halt the ball before it hit Sasha and brought it back to her.

"Why'd you stop?" Sasha lowered her arms.

"You covered your face. You cannot protect yourself if you cannot see what's coming at you." Wendy allowed the ball to float around her once more. "We will try again, and this time you will keep your hands down," Wendy instructed.

"And if my shield fails?"

"Then you will learn for next time," Wendy said.

Sasha swallowed and nodded. "I think I'm ready."

Wendy let the ball float around her a then sent flying toward Sasha.

Sasha clenched her fist to keep them by her side. She focused on the ball flying towards her thought of a glass wall surrounding her, but it was not enough. She hissed as the ball made contact with her forehead sending her back a few steps.

She rubbed the spot quickly once the ball fell. "I learned you need a softer ball."

"Good first try." Wendy clapped ignoring Sasha's comment.

"How?" She asked as she rubbed where the ball hit her, trying to ease the sting.

"Because you slowed it down." Wendy pointed out. "I know the speed I sent it. I saw the resistance once it got close to you. You had a shield, not a strong one but it was there."

"If only it did not hurt as much." Sasha rubbed the sore spot.

"Next time will be better," Wendy assured. She let the ball float around her. "Get ready."

Sasha nodded once more, but a red light started to flash around the room. Wendy's face morphed from concentration to confusion, to anger than determination.

"Follow me!" She ordered running from the room. Sasha didn't question, she just followed. They ran down the hall a couple of steps before crossing down another hall. Sasha had yet to explore during her short time there and stuck close to Wendy to keep from getting lost. The sound of a door slamming caused Sasha to look back over her shoulder. Danny and Devin came running down the hall after them. Danny had Cassie's hand and was pulling her along after him.

Wendy ran into a door on the left, Sasha hot on her trail. The room was full of screens showing off the surrounding wooded area and parts of the hidden home. "What's going on?" Sasha asked once they were all in the room. Cassie immediately reached for Sasha's hand and came to her side.

"Someone is too close!" Wendy scanned the screens looking for movement.

"There!" Devin pointed to one screen. "Two men!"

Wendy typed a few buttons on the

keyboard, and soon all the screens showed the two men, one adult, and one teen. "What are they doing here?" Wendy whispered staring at the screen.

"They could be just hikers," Sasha suggested.

"No, we are way too deep in the forest for that." Danny stared at the screen. "No one comes this deep to hike and technically we are on protected land, so no one is allowed to be here."

"Wait," Cassie came closer to the screen. "I think I know them. Can you get a close up of their faces?" she squinted.

Wendy typed a few more keys, and the image grew larger and then looked back at Cassie. "Who are they?"

"Yeah," she squeezed her eyes shut trying to remember from where she met the two men. "Umm, the older guy he's a friend of my parents...his name is um," she racked her brain. "Cor- Cormac I think and that is his son, but I don't know his name, I never met the son in person before."

"The question is what are they doing here?" Danny looked at her.

She shrugged. "They live like two towns over I think."

"But what are they doing *here*?" Wendy stressed Danny's questions again. "How are they so close to where we are, did you two call anyone."

"No." Sasha shook her head. "We left our phones at the house. We have no way of telling anyone where we are."

"Then why are her parent's friends less than a mile outside my house?" Wendy questioned.

"Hey!" Sasha stood in front of Cassie. "Don't yell at her."

"Last time I saw that man I was like ten." Cassie defended herself. "I have no idea why they are here."

"We need to go talk to them," Danny said. "It's no fluke they are here. Mom, you, me and Cassie go out there and greet them. Devin and Sasha can stay here and follow us on the screen. Devin knows what to do if there is trouble." He nodded to his twin and grabbed Cassie's hand.

"Wait, no!" Sasha pulled Cassie behind her. "If she's goes, then I go."

"No." Wendy shook her head. "Cassie knows them, so she is coming with us. It is not safe to take you out there Sasha."

"No," Sasha stressed. "She is only in this

mess because of me. If I am not safe, neither is she. I am not letting her go alone."

"Sasha no, it is ok..." Cassie stepped forward releasing her hand. "I can do this, I know them."

"But, I should go with you."

"I'll be safe, right?" She looked over her shoulder at Danny who nodded.

"Fine." Sasha conceded after a moment.

"Let's not waste any more time." Wendy grabbed few things from around the room. "Devin you know what to do if this goes wrong."

"Yeah, but I rather not have to use it." He sat down in the chair and started to type a few commands into the computer.

"We all would." Danny grabbed Cassie's hand and followed behind Wendy.

Devin grabbed one of the seats and pushed it over to Sasha then returned to typing on the keyboard. The screens went back to normal showing multiple views of the forest. Sasha watched as Wendy, Danny, and Cassie walked out the secret door and into the woods.

"What will you have to do if things do go wrong?" She asked taking a seat in the offered chair.

"Blow up this section of the mountain," Devin answered not taking his eyes off the screen.

"You're joking right?" Sasha looked at him incredulously.

Devin shook his head. "No, we have an exit through those doors." He pointed behind him. "It leads deeper into the mountain; we have an escape tunnel through there."

"What about them?" she pointed to the screens.

"There are charges in some of the trees; it will cause a distraction allowing them to escape."

"And if the charges don't create a large enough distraction."

"They will," Devin assured her.

"And if they don't, what about Cassie? I can't leave her!" she pressed.

"It's not just your friend out there Sasha; it's my mother and my twin. The plan will work."

Chapter Twelve

Wendy walked slightly ahead of Cassie and Danny leading the way to their destination.

Danny kept a tight grip on Cassie's hand, leading her after his mother.

"We should be close to the pace they were taking," Wendy called from in front of them.

"Is there a reason you are holding my hand so tight?" Cassie whispered to Danny.

"So we all stay together," he whispered back.

"How come you're not holding your mother's hand?" she taunted.

"Because we know these woods and if we were to get separated we could find our way back. You, not so much."

Cassie rolled her eyes at his answer. The forest was thick but not that thick. Anyway, she still interlocked her fingers with his. "Just in case." She smirked at him as he tightened his hold.

They walked for a few minutes until Wendy signaled for them to quiet down. They hid behind the trees and listened to the sounds of footsteps in the forest. Soon the two men in question walked through the brush. The first, Cormac, stood around 6'3-ish with brown hair that cut neatly on his head. He had hard black eyes he squinted as he looked up at the sky.

His son stood a bit taller than him. His hair was darker and longer, with curls that dropped down to his ears.

Cassie made a move to step forward, but Danny grabbed her waist and held her to him.

Once the men were in the center of the clearing, Wendy cleared her throat and stepped forward. Cormac and his son stopped as they spotted her. Cassie felt Danny tense up behind her when Cormac signaled to his son.

"What are you doing here?" Wendy asked.

Cormac stepped forward. "Hello, we are just looking for a friend. We are not looking for any trouble."

"Why are you so far onto my property?"

"I apologize I did not realize this was

private property. Let me start over." He paused. "My name is Cormac Cavazos, and this is my son Derek. We are friends of the Lightworths. We are looking for their daughter Cassandra. They gave us her GPS location, and we were just following the coordinates here."

"How would her parents have her GPS location?" Wendy questioned.

"They have a GPS tracker on her."

Cassie tensed at his words. *Her parents were tracking her.*

"Did you know about this?" Danny whispered in her ear. Cassie shook her head no.

Wendy tucked her hair behind her ear, a signal to Danny to stay put.

"Look, I'll be honest," Cormac held up his hands in surrender. "I know who you are and I'm going to guess it's not a coincidence she's in this area. I want you to know we are on your side and we just want to protect her. We want to make sure she is ok. As you can imagine her parents are worried about her."

Wendy ran her fingers through her hair signaling again. Cassie felt Danny step back and grab her arm and they walked up behind Wendy.

"Cassandra," Cormac smiled laying eyes on the young woman. "I am very pleased to see you, and I know your parents will be as well."

"Why do her parents have a tracker on her?" Danny asked from beside her. "And where is it?"

"They are in her earrings, and they are for her protection," Cormac answered. "This situation is a perfect example of why they have them in. Is Sasha and Jasmine with you?" he glanced around to the surrounding area.

Cassie's hand rubbed the diamond studs her parent gave for her fourteenth birthday. They were her favorite, and she rarely took them off.

"Normal parents just track their child's cell phones." Wendy pointed out. "Why do they have trackers in their daughter's earrings? And how do you know who I am and that I'm not my sister?"

Cormac pulled out a phone and tossed it to Cassie who hastily caught it. "It is not just my secret to tell, they are waiting for your call, and they will answer any questions you may have."

Cassie looked to Wendy for the ok. She

nodded, and Cassie dialed her parent's number and placed the call on speaker.

The phone rang a few times in the open air before her mother's frantic voice answered. "Cormac! Did you find her? Is she safe, is she ok?"

"Mom!" Cassie exclaimed clutching the phone tighter.

"Cassie!" her mother cried in relief. "John it's Cassie she's on the phone, come quickly." She yelled away from the phone before coming back. "Darling are you ok? Are you safe? Are Sasha and Jasmine with you?"

"Mom," Cassie sniffed. "I'm fine and so is Sasha but Mom, Jasmine's not with us. She gave herself up; she told us to go on without her. She did it so Sasha and I could get away. She sent us to her sister's house."

"Ok," Cathy breathed. "But you two are safe; she would want that. I need to speak to Wendy."

Cassie paused and looked to Wendy, who held out her hand for the phone. Cassie handed it over. "This is Wendy."

"Thank you for keeping her safe," Cathy said.

"You are welcome," Wendy said. "But I

have a few questions. Why do you have a tracker on Cassie? A tracker that my equipment should have picked up but did not. Also, why would you send your friends to find her and not Enforcers? And last, how do you know my name? Cassie never said it." Her eyes were trained on Cormac. She was ready to make a move it need be.

They heard a bit a whispering and rummaging on the other side of the phone.

"Mom?" Cassie asked after a bit a silence.

"Cassie, darling we should have never kept this from you. We never expected it to matter anymore until a few years ago. We were dormant for so long." Cathy's voice rang out in the clearing. "Our family was, well we are a part of an old group, we are descendants from a set of Royal Guards. For years we have been watching Jasmine's family. Always there adding an extra layer of protection. We have been watching over Jasmine and Sasha since they moved to our town. Cormac and his family are a part of that group as well. Which is why we sent them. We know them, and we can trust them."

"My parents told us about you guys, but they never said who you were. Did Jasmine know about you?" Wendy asked.

"She never mentioned she knew it was us. But I always suspected she knew we were a part of the group. Her late husband Sam was one of us. He got her to move here after the incident because he was aware that there were people in town that could protect her. But he never told her who we were, and she never wanted to know." John took over the conversation. "When we saw how far the girls traveled we were not sure if it was by force or choice. Cormac agreed to investigate it for us. To see if you were friend or foe." John went on to explained. "We are pleased to know it's you, Wendy. That you are alive and well."

"Well I am not a fan of surprises, but I will admit this does answer a problem we have. If they are here for Cassie, it does help the plan to get her back to you. But I would rather they 'find' her near their town to keep the trail away from my home." Wendy explained, and Cassie felt Danny grab her hand once more.

"They cannot bring Cassie home yet." John sighed into the phone.

"Wait... what, why?" Cassie asked.

"We do not think it's safe for you to be found yet. With the turn in the news about Jasmine, the Royal Enforcers have come to town, and something seems off. Our contacts tell us they are just here to funnel all the information about the case in through them. Your mother and I think it would be best, safer if they do not know where you are."

"So it's all true then," Cassie sighed. "What Wendy told us that Sasha and Jasmine are the real Royal Family and what we heard on the news?"

"Yes," Cathy chimed in.

"What are we supposed to do then?" Cassie asked.

"Stay hidden. We need to wait this out until we know it's safe for you to come home." Cathy explained.

"I guess." Cassie's shoulders dropped a bit.

"Wendy?" Cathy asked, "If it is possible we have a friend who is close by, he is willing to protect the girls for us. We understand you are Sasha's aunt, but we would like a bit more protection given the recent attack. They may know where you are."

"I will not allow Sasha to move. Not when so many eyes are looking for them. My house is protection enough. We are completely off the grid; they are plenty safe here." Wendy countered.

"I know, I understand but please." Cathy's voice pleaded from the phone. "I would rather not separate the girls right now. John and I would feel much better if Cassie was somewhere we are familiar with."

"Your daughter is safe here," Wendy assured her again.

"And we do not doubt that." John's voice came through. "But we are her parents, and we want her somewhere we are comfortable with; it will give us more peace of mind."

Wendy sighed, "I can't stop you from taking your daughter. You are her parents, and it's your right to protect her any way you see fit. Jasmine wanted me to protect Sasha; I won't allow her to leave." Wendy explained.

"Then I'm not leaving!" Cassie interrupted. "If Sasha stays so do I!"

"Cassie, what is going on is so much

bigger than you can understand. Your protection is the most important thing to your mother and I. We know you will be safe with Cormac." John explained.

Cassie shook her head and looked to Wendy. "I'm not leaving Sasha, and you're not here to make me."

"Cassie your parents just want to protect you. I can't risk moving Sasha right now." Wendy tried to let the young girl down softly.

"No!" Cassie screamed. "Sasha is my sister; we've been through everything together. I won't be forced to leave her when she needs me the most!"

"Wendy," Cormac spoke up. "Cassie's parents would never do anything to put her in danger; you know Sasha will be safe. How about we come up with a compromise? Come with us just for a few days. Just to see where we will be."

Wendy shook her head. "I will not move my family to a home that I am not familiar with." She repeated Cathy's words.

"Mom, is it a bad idea?" Danny spoke up.

"Yes," she glared at her son. "You need to understand, Cassie's end game is to make it back to her parents, Sasha will not have that chance. Moving her is not smart when she needs to stay hidden." Wendy sighed. "I know you don't want to leave her Cassie, but you have the chance of making it back your family. Sasha is where she needs to be; this is where Jasmine intended for her to come."

"I know that but…" Cassie tried to argue.

"Cassie, moving Sasha is not in her best interest, it will only expose her further."

"Then I'm not going," Cassie said defiantly.

"Cassie," Cathy warned.

"No Mom, you were not there when they attacked, you didn't see what it did to her when her Mom put us in the tunnel. To find out everything she thought she knew was a lie. I'm not leaving her if you take me I will just come back. If Sasha doesn't go neither will I."

"Cassie..." Wendy started.

"How about you think it over, Wendy?" Derek, Cormac's son, suggested cutting in. "It is getting late; too late to head back tonight away. My dad and I will be camping in the area for the night. Take some time and think it over and if tomorrow you don't want to come with us then, we will discuss it then."

"We are fine with that," Cathy answered after a moment.

"I will allow you to camp out here tonight while I do a bit a research." She turned to Cassie. "Take off your earrings," Wendy ordered holding out her hand. Cassie quickly reached up and took off each one and placed them in Wendy's hand. "I will let you know in the morning. Is this agreeable?"

Cassie bit her lip but nodded.

"We agree. Thank you." Cormac said.

"Yes, thank you." John's voice came through the phone. "Cassie, we know you are upset, but this is what is best, we love you."

"I love you too," Cassie replied in a small voice.

"We will talk tomorrow," John said ending the call. Cassie handed it back to Cormac.

"Here." Wendy handed the earrings over to Cormac. "I will not have those in my home anymore." She said then started back towards her home. Danny grabbed Cassie's hand and gave one last look at the two men and headed after his mother.

They walked in silence until they reached the hidden door. The door opened, and Devin and Sasha stood there waiting for them.

"What happened out there?" Devin asked.

"They are camping in the area," Wendy said. "I need to do a bit research on them."

"Did they explain how they found us?" Devin asked.

"My parents sent them," Cassie explained. "To take us to safety if it was needed."

"I saw you take off your earrings," Sasha said. "Why?"

"My parents put a tracker in them," Cassie explained.

"What, why?" Sasha asked.

"They know about you guys. About everything Wendy told us. They were in the town to protect you and your mother." Cassie explained as they walked down to their room.

"Sasha you need to say something," Cassie said once they entered their shared room, since her last statement, she had yet to utter a word.

"I don't know what to say?" Sasha shook her head. "Why are you not more freaked out.?"

"I am," Cassie admitted. She reached up to the vacant spot where her earrings used to be. "Trust me I am. They want us to leave."

"Leave and go where?" Sasha asked.

"They have a friend that doesn't live too far from here. He has a place where I can stay and be protected."

"But we are protected here?" Sasha said.

"I know, I told them that. But I can't get over the fact that they knew about this. They knew about you and your mom. Like everything in the story, Wendy told us. They've known who you were all along. Your Dad was a part of it too. That's why they moved to Blanton."

"What?" Sasha leaned back on her bed.

"They are all descendants of the guards who were loyal to your great grandmother. They've watched over your family for years."

"No...No!," Sasha shook her head. She refused to believe what her friend was telling her.

"Yeah, so they sent their friends here to

come and protect me on the journey to their other friend's house."

"Has anyone in our life not lied to us?" Sasha asked.

"Doesn't seem like it." Cassie shook her head.

"So where are we going?" Sasha asked.

"No Sasha." Cassie dropped her shoulders. "Not us, I said me...just me," she whispered the last word.

"What, no, they can't do that!"

"Wendy doesn't want you to go since your mother planned for you to be here anyway. She does not see the point in moving you."

"But we just got here; you can't leave yet." Sasha reasoned.

"I know, but my parents want me to be somewhere they know. I tried to talk them out of it but... they, of course, they are not listening to me. I told them I'm not leaving without you," she shook her head.

"Cassie..."

"No." She shook her head firmly. "I'm not leaving you."

"Cassie you can't," Sasha said. "As much I don't want you to leave, you were always going to go home."

"Yeah, I knew that, but I never expected to so soon. Sasha, I can't." There was a knock on the door, and Wendy poked her head in the door. "I need to speak to you two." She stepped in, closing the door behind her.

"Cassie already told me what happened out there," Sasha said wiping away the tears that started to fall without her permission.

Wendy nodded. "I figured as much." She walked around the room. "I want you girls to know that I am not taking this lightly."

"I don't want to leave yet." Cassie pleaded. "Please don't make me go."

"Cassie." Wendy took a seat on Cassie's bed. "I am not making a decision, but you have to understand. I am not comfortable with anyone knowing where my family is. Your parents want you protected. As a mother myself, I have to respect their decision."

"It's not their decision to make! I am not a child. I survived people trying to kill me because Sasha and I were together! We survived the trip here because we were together. We are stronger together."

"They are your parents."

"Who've lied to me my entire life. I

don't know what to think right now. And to be around more strangers who have had a part in their lives, that alone doesn't make me feel safe. Like I told them if they force me leave I will just come back." Cassie said defiantly.

"Cassie."

"No, I've made my decision. I'm not leaving."

"We will talk tomorrow." Wendy stood seeing she was not going to get through to the girls tonight.

Chapter Thirteen

Sasha turned in the chair watching the many screens. Most of them focused on Cormac and his son Derek. Danny sat down next to her as Cassie had just left to get something to drink. Wendy's rule, no liquids in this room ever.

Devin was missing from the observation party - he was busy training with Wendy for the rest of the afternoon. When Sasha asked why Danny said it was to make sure they were in tip top shape in case they could not trust their next visitor.

According to them, Cormac and Derek were there for their protection. Sasha watched the younger one, Derek, put up the tent. They had powers, but he was doing it the long way, she noted. In the process of putting up the tent, he had shed his heavy backpack and his outer jacket. His t-shirt was pulled tight against his forearms, and his face had a deep look of concentration up as he put the finishing touches on the tent.

"Stop staring so hard." Danny laughed pulling Sasha out of her thoughts.

"What?" She looked to him.

Danny snorted. "I said stop staring so hard."

"I don't know what you're talking about?" Sasha shook her head and leaned back in her chair.

"Yeah, right. If you stare any harder you, would fall through the screen and right into his arms."

"I *said* I don't know what you are talking about."

"Ok, whatever you say." Danny rolled his eyes.

"I wasn't staring." She murmured as she scanned the different screens... the ones that didn't have Derek on them.

"What are they up to?" Wendy asked walking in, wiping sweat from her brow.

"Just setting up the camp," Danny answered. "I haven't seen them call anyone, but they could have when we were walking back here."

Wendy pulled out the chair next to Sasha, sat down, and started typing into a small laptop there.

"What are you doing?" Sasha asked.

"Looking into their backgrounds," Wendy answered never taking her eyes off the screen. In a few clicks, the screen was full of Cormac's life. "Cassie's parents might trust them, that does not mean I do."

"But they wouldn't send someone they didn't trust." Sasha reasoned.

"Sasha," Wendy explained. "I learned a long time ago never to take someone else's word on who to trust."

Sasha nodded but didn't say anything. She just watched as photos of their family and their history strolled across the screen. She watched as pictures of Derek flashed across the screen. All from different periods of time.

She had to admit he was adorable as a child and grew into quite a looker. She shook her head at the thought. She was not attracted to this boy. To someone, she never met… in person. She watched Wendy fly through the screen; page after page, photo after photo. There was no way she was reading it all that fast.

A few minutes later, Cassie and Devin joined them. Devin toweled off his hair. "What did you find?" he stood behind his mother reading over her shoulder.

"So far everything looks clean."

"Wait are you looking into them?" Cassie asked. "Why? My parents trust them."

"I need to know for myself," Wendy answered.

Cassie nodded and walked over to Danny, leaning on the part of the desk near him ignoring the questioning look she got from Sasha.

"So what do you think we should do?" Cassie asked.

"I have not come to a clear answer. Though Danny and Devin have pointed out a valid point, I might have missed."

"What type of point?" Sasha leaned forward.

"We need allies, with Jasmine taken we need more people we can rely on for safety."

"So you are letting Sasha come with me tomorrow?" Cassie asked leaning forward.

"No." Wendy shook her head still typing away.

"Oh." Cassie leaned back.

"No one is leaving tomorrow?" Wendy clarified. " I will talk it over with Cormac and your parents in the morning. I will see if they are willing to stay here for a few more days. I need to get to know them for myself. I would also like to speak to their contact to know where you are going. If everything checks out, in a few days' time, we will all journey there."

"So there is a chance?" Cassie perked up.

"Yes. Only if everything adds up. It will do my sons good to know another safe place if need be."

"So about how much time do you need to think it over?" Sasha asked.

"About two days, three days at the most. I know you trust your parents Cassie, but I still need time to think this over."

"No, I get it!" Cassie nodded.

"Thanks." Sasha smiled.

"Don't thank me yet," Wendy said. "Nothing is set in stone yet. I said only if everything checks out."

"Not a definite yes…" Cassie winked to Sasha.

"But not a no." Sasha smiled back.

Chapter Fourteen

Sasha yawned as she walked into the living room early the next morning; stretching her arms high trying to wake up her body.

"Morning," Derek said from his spot on the couch surprising Sasha.

"Morning." She dropped her hands to her sides pulling her night shirt lower over her stomach. "What are you doing in here?" she looked around for Wendy or some type of explanation. He was laying on the couch, his shoes off and his feet up on the arm rest. He was wearing a different pair of shorts and a different shirt from what she saw on the screen yesterday. This one was a white tee shirt, but it was as tight as the shirt he was wearing yesterday. She was able to make out the muscles of his arms.

"Wendy came to the camp site this morning and invited us here." He explained pulling her out of her thoughts. "I think Wendy is talking to my Dad."

"Oh," She nodded.

"Am I in your way?" he started to get off the couch.

"No," she shook her head back out of the room. "I should start on breakfast; I'm a bit hungry."

"Need any help?"

"No, it's going to be simple. I'm thinking maybe oatmeal or cream of wheat. You know simple." She grimaced, realizing she repeated herself.

"If it turns out not to be so simple I'm here if you need help." He smiled.

She nodded and backed out the room and walked down the hall to the kitchen. Wendy stood against the kitchen counter with a cup of steaming coffee in her hand. She was talking to Cormac who stood opposite her with a cup of coffee in his hand as well.

"Sasha you're up." Wendy smiled as Sasha stepped into the room.

"Yeah, I couldn't sleep that well. You know with everything going on."

Wendy gave her a small smile and placed her coffee cup on the counter beside her. "I know what you are going through. I went through it myself. If you want to talk about it, we can."

"Thanks, but not yet." She answered. "I'm still trying to wrap my head around everything, but I think I will take you up on that later."

"Just let me know." Wendy picked up her cup and took another sip of coffee. Sasha herself was more of a tea drinker. "I do have something to talk to you about," Wendy said placing the cup down once more. "Cormac and I have been talking. He would like to aid in your training."

"Really?" Sasha turned to him.

Cormac nodded. "Your powers should have never been kept from you. It would be my honor to help you learn to control them."

"Thank you, when do you want to start?"

"No time like the present." He finished off the rest of his coffee pushed off the kitchen counter.

"Now?" Sasha asked startled. "Like now...now?" She rubbed her grumbling stomach. She was hoping to get something to eat sooner rather than later.

"Yes, I'm not sure how long Wendy will allow Derek and me to stay. I would like to use as much time as I can to teach you everything that I can."

"Let her eat first Cormac otherwise I

don't think she will be any good," Wendy said coming to Sasha's aide.

"Say thirty minutes?"

"Thirty minutes." Sasha agreed.

"I think I remember where you told me the gym was," he placed his cup in the sink. "I will see you in thirty minutes, Sasha." He said walking out of the room.

As soon as he was out of ear shot, Sasha turned to Wendy. "So you trust them now?" she asked.

"I'm not sure if I trust them, but I did speak to Cassie's parents last night. They trust him, and I am trusting them not to put their daughter in any danger. Also, my check into their lives matches up. No red flags in the last couple of weeks."

"Do you have an answer about going to their friend's house? Since you know everything is on the up and up?" Sasha smiled walking through the kitchen trying to figure out what to eat.

"Not yet. It's a bit harder to get any real info on him. I need to know all the facts before I can make a decision that affects all of our lives."

"I understand," Sasha sighed. "But same with Cormac and Derek, Cassie parents wouldn't send us somewhere that wasn't safe for us. They've known me my entire life. They would never do anything that would hurt their daughter or me."

"I know, I know, but I need to find out for myself. I need a reason to trust them other than the fact someone else trusts them."

"Fine." Sasha relented realizing she was not going to get through to her aunt this way.

"Now eat up," Wendy suggested. "Who knows what he has planned for your first training session."

Chapter Fifteen

Sasha rolled her shoulders as she walked into the training room to meet with Cormac.

"Thirty minutes on the dot. Good." He said as he looked down at his watch. "We can start."

"What are we starting with?" Sasha asked walking to the center of the mat.

"I talked it over with Wendy this morning. She told me that you two worked on moving objects and it went pretty good for your first try." He complimented. "So today I thought that we could work on prolonging your strength."

"What would you like me to do?" Sasha asked, excitement flooding her body.

Cormac nodded to some small rubber balls laying on the ground. "I think the most important aspect for you is to work on your shield strength."

"What about being able to attack? I mean after what happened at my house, I would like to work on that."

Cormac shook his head. "Not necessary at the moment, but we will work on it at a later date. I think right now you need to know how to protect yourself for longer periods of time."

Sasha nodded. She guessed that made sense.

"Create a shield." He instructed, and Sasha focused on a creating her shield around her. He watched as a light green bubble started to form around her.

"Ready." She said once she felt it was strong enough....well she hoped it was strong enough.

Cormac lifted the balls in the air and sent them flying towards Sasha.

They bounced on the shield leaving cracks in their wake. "Fix them!" Cormac ordered sending the attack from all sides.

Sasha felt her magic rush out and fill the cracks Cormac kept making. At some point, he switched from the small rubber balls to energy balls. They weren't as strong as the ones she encountered at her house, but they were enough to do damage. The energy balls slammed into her shield, and the force of the impact slid her back a few inches. A long crack formed right down the middle of her shield. She took a breath and repaired it best she could but the stronger she made it, the more she felt her energy depleting.

Her legs shook as she fought to keep up the strength of her shield as Cormac sent another round of energy blast towards her.

"Good." Cormac praised sending a few more small energy balls towards her.

Sasha's legs shook after the last wave, and she dropped to her knees. The shield wavered before shattering at the last impact sending her into the wall behind her.

She slowly lifted her body into a sitting position and held her head in her hands.

"Are you ok?" Cormac rushed to her side helping her to a standing position.

"Yeah I think so…" she rubbed her neck and leaned back on the wall for support. "But I could go for a nap right now."

"This was a good first step, a great practice. But I did hope your strength level would be a bit higher."

"This is only my second day; I will improve," Sasha assured him, though she had a feeling it was mostly for herself.

"Of that, I have complete faith." He patted her on the back. "We will keep working on it. The only way for you to get stronger is to keep practicing."

"But not right now, I need a nap." She laughed.

"We'll meet up after lunch, this was just for me to see what you could do for myself." he suggested walking her to the door.

"After lunch....today?"

"Yes, as I told you, your aunt has not given her answer so I would like to get as much training in with you as possible."

"That's true but I..."

"Dad there you are," Derek said as he entered the room, holding a phone. "Mom's on the line."

"Thank you," Cormac took the phone from Derek. "Can you make sure Sasha makes it back to her room, the workout might have been too much for her." He didn't bother waiting for a response already engrossed in the conversation with his wife. They took that a sign and walked out the room.

"Hey." Sasha leaned against the wall once they were alone. "Umm... you don't have to help me back to my room."

"It's no problem," Derek shrugged. "I think I'm heading that way." He laughed as she pushed off the wall but quickly reached her arm out to steady herself. "Plus I do think you need help." He wrapped his arm around her waist and pulled her to him.

They walked down the hall in silence and Sasha became very aware of how close they were to each other. His arm gripped her waist tightly keeping her upright. All things considered, he smelled amazing... at least for a guy. His cinnamon smell filled her stomach with butterflies. Crap, She wondered. Did she smell, is that why he wasn't talking. She did just get out a training session. Not a long one but she still worked up a sweat. Also, she did not shower the night before or this morning. She knew she would be training this morning. He was a guy, and he had to know that right...She shook her head trying to stop her train of thought. This was not the time to start liking someone...no matter how much he affected her.

Chapter Sixteen

Robert sat down in his favorite recliner chair as George and Kaitlin made themselves comfortable across from him.

"Something is not right in this town," he started, "and I am ready for some real answers and not whatever Hunter and his men will try to shove down our throats. Kaitlin, what did you find on the laptop?"

"Not much more than what I told you at her house," Kaitlin sighed. "But I was able to see what she was working on last. She was finishing up a report of this week about Jasmine and Sasha's life. There was nothing in the report about the attack. I think whenever she was killed, it had to be close to when she got home from Jasmine's house. The issue I'm having is I still can't figure out who she was sending the reports to. From the way the computer is set up, after she sent each report she crashed it then reinstalled everything. You only do that if you want to make sure no one would have an easy time finding who you are talking to. Based on the most recent report, I figure whoever is receiving the reports wants to know about Jasmine's everyday life. I printed out a copy of the report." She handed them both a copy and both men skimmed it.

"It reads like what a wife would tell their husband about their day."

"I know, but I doubt Jasmine knew what Susan was doing," Kaitlin added.

"It makes you wonder how Susan's death fits into all of this," Robert said. "It sounds like she was not here to do Jasmine any harm, but she was here to look after her."

"Well, I should have mentioned this earlier." She reached down and took her laptop out of her bag. "I was able to clone her laptop before I gave it to Hunter. I found the IP address of who she was sending the report to."

"Where was it?" Robert pushed.

"The IP address came from the Royal Castle."

"The Castle?" George asked. "Like the Royal Family?"

"Yeah, which is weird right," Kaitlin said.

"Well it doesn't necessarily mean it's the Royal Family, it just means she's communicating with someone at the castle. There are hundreds of people who work at the castle; it could be anyone." George said.

"It would explain why the Royal Enforcers arrived so quickly," Robert stated.

"If this is true, we are stepping into a total nightmare," George said. "This means an undercover operation went dangerously wrong resulting in the attack on two innocent girls who are now missing. I doubt they would want bad press. It would look bad for them no matter how it turned out."

"Which is why they sent the Royal Enforcers to take over the case. They are here to handle any sensitive information." Robert agreed.

"Does this mean we stop working on the case?" Kaitlin asked.

Robert shook his head. "No, if anything it means we work harder to find the truth."

"But if Jasmine did attack the crown then she does deserve to be taken in," Kaitlin said.

"From what I gathered from those who knew her, she was not the type of person to do this," Robert explained.

"But she is the kind of person who would keep the fact she was magical a secret from everyone who knew her. Or thought they knew her. George, you were close to the family. What do you make of it?" Kaitlin turned to him.

"I don't know." He shook her head. "I knew she was hiding something but I just never would have guessed it was something like this."

"But you're an Enforcer!" Kaitlin argued. "How can you be friends with her for so long and not know?"

"I wasn't looking," he defended himself. "But hey I was only close to Sam, her husband. After he died, I mostly just checked in on them to make sure they were OK. Jasmine wasn't that friendly with me."

"I still think you should have noticed something," Kaitlin muttered.

"That's not the issue." Robert cut in. "Jasmine wanted to stay hidden. People like that make sure they blend in. I don't fault George for not looking too deep into his friends' past. It looks like she never gave anyone a reason to look."

"Well, where do we go from here?" Kaitlin asked.

"We keep our heads down and pay attention to what Hunter and his men are doing. If they are here to cover up the story, we can't let that happen. And most of all, no matter what Jasmine did, Sasha and Cassie are still two innocent victims who might need saving."

Chapter Seventeen

"You think he's cute!" Cassie flopped on Sasha's bed once Derek was out of hearing range.

"What are you talking about?" Sasha said as she flopped down beside Cassie.

"Derek, you like him," Cassie stated as she nodded towards the door.

Sasha rolled her eyes. "I still have no idea what you're talking about."

"I know you, and I know the way you looked at him. I know you like him."

"He's attractive." Sasha conceded. "But it's not like he's going to be around for much longer."

"So get what you can while you can."

"I can't with you." Sasha laughed.

"You can and will and always do." Cassie climbed on top of her and wrapped her around her body giving her a bear hug.

"Ugh get off me." Sasha pushed her. "I'm tired, and I want to take a nap."

Cassie ignored Sasha's weak attempts to

get away and tightened her hold. "Not until you admit it."

"Why? What's the big deal?" Sasha whined.

"Because " Cassie exclaimed like it was obvious. "Sasha as long as I've know you you've never liked a guy. Sure, you thought they were cute, but you've never liked one. No one's ever caught your eye like him."

"Well sorry to burst your crazy bubble, I don't know him well enough to like him."

"It doesn't matter." Cassie shook her head. "You have time to get to know him, and the spark is there. Plus," she lowered her voice, "I saw the way he had looked at you before he left the room. He was checking you out."

"He was?" The question slipped from Sasha's mouth, and she regretted it the moment she saw the satisfied smirk that crawled across Cassie's face.

"See I knew it!" She rolled back to her knees and fist pumped.

"Knew what?" Danny asked as he entered the girl's bedroom.

"We have a door." Sasha rolled her eyes.

"In my house…" Danny retorted taking a seat on Cassie's bed. "But that doesn't answer my question," He turned to Cassie. "What did you know?"

Cassie climbed off Sasha's bed and walked over to Danny who reached out and grabbed her hand once she was close enough. "I knew that Sasha liked Derek and vice versa." She smiled.

"Oh, I saw that coming a mile away." Danny played with Cassie's fingers.

Sasha rolled over to face them. "How?"

"The way you stared at him through the monitors…and the way he looks at you."

"That doesn't mean anything." Sasha deflected.

Danny shrugged. "I wouldn't say that I'm a guy and I know how guys work; he looked at you like he wanted you."

"And how sure are you about that?" Sasha asked.

"It was the same look I had when I saw this one." He pulled Cassie closer to him. "So I am pretty sure."

"You know I have a name." Cassie rolled her eyes.

"Ok, enough of you two making eyes at each other. I just want to take a nap, so can you take this to your room, Derek." Sasha pulled her covers over her missing her mistake

"First of all" Danny smiled. "My name is Danny, and I would go to my room, but my brother is in there working on something he calls very important, and he wants peace and quiet."

Sasha ignored his remark and her slip up. "Then the living room Just gets out, I'm tired, and I have another training session this afternoon, and I would like to sleep before it."

"Oh, will Derek be there?" Cassie asked, Danny, stood up and started pulling her to the door.

"Get out!" Sasha yelled.

"I'm just asking." Cassie laughed as they left the room shutting the door behind them.

Sasha shook her head and smiled as she drifted off to sleep with thoughts of a particular guy filling her dreams.

Chapter Eighteen

"Hey, sleepy head..." Cassie sang once Sasha walked into the kitchen.

"Hey," Sasha looked around the room. Danny and Devin were talking in the corner. Cassie was helping Wendy prepare their lunch which looked like sandwiches. Her stomach rumbled loudly at the thought of food.

"I hear someone is hungry." Wendy quipped placing a plate on the table. "Cormac told me you two were training again after lunch; here you need your strength."

"Thank you." Sasha slid in the chair and started eating.

"How did your first session go with Cormac?" Wendy pushed in the seat next to her.

"She did well." Cormac walked in the kitchen, Derek behind him. Sasha caught Derek's eye but quickly diverted her eyes to her plate as she felt her face heat up.

Cassie slid in the chair next to her bumping shoulders with her. "Feeling a bit flushed Sasha?" Cassie giggled.

"Shut up." Sasha hissed under her breath taking another bite of her sandwich.

"What's your plan for this afternoon?" Wendy asked as they joined the table.

"We worked on her shields this morning, so this afternoon I would like to see her attacks." Cormac grabbed a plate and placed a sandwich on it. "I will try to cover the basics as much as I can before we leave...Have you given any more thought to our offer?"

"I have, but I'm not ready to give you an answer. I have a few more options to think over." Wendy explained.

Cormac nodded and didn't push further. Danny and Devin leaned against the counters while the others ate around the table.

"So Derek, tell us about yourself?" Cassie asked ignoring the pinch on her leg from Sasha.

"What do you want to know?" he asked his eyes never leaving Sasha.

"Umm, I don't know." She feigned innocence. "How old are you? What do you do for fun? Likes and dislikes? You know…the basics." She leaned on her palms. "We want to know more about you."

"Umm, ok." Derek paused. "I'm eighteen; I run for fun…"

"You like running?" Cassie cut in. "Are you crazy?"

"No just active." Derek retorted.

"Sasha likes to run…or she's good at it. She's fast." Cassie said ignoring the extra pinch Sasha gave her. "When we were in the tunnel, I was about to die of exhaustion, but for Sasha, it was like a cake walk."

"Cassie shut up." Sasha seethed.

"What!" Cassie protested. "I'm just trying to get to know the guy, I mean I will be leaving with them in a few days. I just want to know who I will be with."

"You are so annoying." Sasha mouthed.

"You love me!" Cassie mouthed back then stuck out her tongue.

"I'll be in the training room." Sasha nodded toward Cormac and left the room.

"You shouldn't mess with her," Devin said taking her seat.

"What? It's not like I have the rest of my life to, we only have a few days left together. I need to make sure she gets the full experience." She laughed.

"I don't understand you," Devin said.

"You're not meant to." Cassie winked at Danny who shook his head with a smile.

Chapter Twenty

Sasha stared at the ceiling twirling her foot in a circle as she waited for Cormac to show.

Her rumbling stomach alerted her to the fact that in her haste to leave the kitchen, and her embarrassment, she never finished her meal. '*Stupid Cassie,*' she thought as she rolled her eyes. It was her fault she didn't finish eating. With her not so subtle way of trying to get to know Derek.

Her stomach rumbled again, and she groaned, this wasn't going to be a fun training session on a nearly empty stomach.

"Nice view?" Derek said walking in the training room carrying a wrapped package. Sasha hoped it was a wrapped up sandwich. She sat up to face him as he held out the wrapped item to her.

"What is it?"

"A sandwich," He answered. "I noticed you left without finishing yours."

"Thanks." She unwrapped it and took a

bite. "Where's your father?"

Derek shrugged. "I think he is still talking to Wendy. She had a few questions to ask him about the group."

"Oh... What is the deal with that group anyway?" she took another bite.

Derek sat down across from her. "We are the Royal Guards; our family has always been there to protect yours."

"That doesn't make any sense." She shook her head. "You've never met me before this. Why would you care for so long?"

"Your aunt told you about your family's origins right?" he leaned back on his hands.

Sasha nodded and finished her sandwich in two more quick bites.

"Well, we are related to Gabriela's personal guards. We've haven't grown much over the years, but our duty has always been the same, to keep your family safe."

"Like some secret society," she laughed.

"I guess you could call it that." He nodded. "Ever since I could remember I've known that my job was to protect you."

"Why? I mean what happened, happened generations ago, why would they still care today? I mean why attack us then and now?"

"You don't know?" he tilted his head at her.

"Know what?" she asked.

"The reason they found your family those years ago was because of your mother," Derek explained.

"My...Mom?"

"Well yeah," he said. "Your mom went to work at the castle. I don't know if she tried to kill them, but I do know she's the reason your family was found back then."

"You don't know my Mom, so stop acting as you do. If she worked at the castle, then she had a good reason."

"Sasha, the crown had no idea you guys even existed. If it had not been for your Mom, they still wouldn't know."

"Well if all of this is her fault why are you and your father here to protect us? Why not just leave and let us fend for ourselves." Sasha retorted.

"Because it is our duty," Derek answered. "We are bound to protect your family, and we are glad to. I mean I get to protect a princess."

"I'm not a princess" Sasha rolled her eyes.

"Yes, you are."

"Even if I was it's not like you would be a guard, so why do you care?"

Derek leaned forward, and Sasha felt her face flush under his stare. "We do it because we believe in it."

"But what's left to believe in?" she whispered.

He leaned forward his lips a breath away. "You," he winked then pulled back and left the room without a second glance.

Sasha watched him leave with wide eyes; she touches her lips where she could still feel the warmth of his breath 'he almost kissed me.'

Cormac entered the room before Sasha could decide what to do next and Sasha quickly cleared her head of any more thoughts.

Though one thought did remain, and she was going to talk to Wendy the first chance she got. Was all of this her mother's fault?

Chapter Twenty-One

"Is it true?" Sasha barged into Wendy's room.

Wendy closed the book she was reading and looked up at Sasha. "This is my bedroom Sasha; I would appreciate you knocking first." Wendy placed her book down on her small table. Wendy's room was larger than hers, but that was not surprising since this was her home. Wendy's room backed up right to the inside wall of the mountain, and she kept the natural tone in the décor of the room. She had a queen-sized bed, and the headboard faced the door.

Sasha guessed it was to make sure she had the best vantage point to the door even while she slept. Along the mountain wall there was a chair and a desk in the position where her back was facing the wall. Again to make sure she had a clear sight of the door.

There was an arm chair pushed into the corner that Wendy was currently sitting in and small end table in front of it.

"Is it true?" Sasha repeated her hand on her hips

Wendy closed her eyes and rubbed the bridge of her nose; once she realized Sasha wasn't going to apologize for barging into her room. "Is what true Sasha?"

"Did they, the Royals, not know about us until my Mom went to work at the castle?" Sasha asked.

Wendy dropped her head, and her silence filled the room giving Sasha all the answer she needed.

"It is," Sasha whispered. "This is my Mom's fault."

"Sasha, it's a bit more complicated."

"But the truth is, if she never went to the castle, we would have never been found."

"Well, yes."

"You lied to me!" she yelled.

"I did not lie."

"Yes, you did. You let me believe she had nothing to do with the attack. You told me you didn't know how they found us."

"It was best that way. I didn't want you to blame her."

"But it is her fault," Sasha confirmed.

"Your mother," Wendy leaned forward.

"She didn't want an ordinary life. She wanted the life that was stolen from us. The life of a Royal. It didn't go as planned and it leads to the death of our family. After that she changed, she wanted to hide out as we had before. It was for the better."

"So what I heard on the radio was true, she did try to kill the Royal Family?"

"Your mother is a lot of things, but she is not a killer. Her plan was never to kill them."

"Then what did she intend to do?" she paced the room.

"She told me it was to find proof of what they did to us," Wendy said. "I tried to talk her out of it; told her it was dangerous, and I was right. I didn't forgive her for a long time. Her actions led to the murder of what little family we had. If she kept her head down like the rest of us, you could have grown up with us all. You could have grown up with family."

"How was she caught?" Sasha asked.

"She never told me," Wendy explained. "All I've ever known is what she said to me in that ten-second phone call. And I quote, 'I've been found out. They know who I am and who you guys are, run now.' I didn't lie when I said I wasn't home during the attack. It was years before my sister and I found each other again, and long before I actually forgave her."

"You could have told me; you should have told me," Sasha whispered.

"No," she shook her head. "The last thing she wanted was for you to know her mistake."

Sasha dropped on Wendy's bed lost in the new information.

"Sasha," she called after a few seconds. "I planned to tell everyone at dinner, but I will tell you now. I've decided that we will go with them to Brandon Baron's home. I know from experience it is not easy to set up a good safe house from scratch. Doing this," she gestured to her home, "all by myself was hard. So, just in case we ever get that call in the night to run, I want you guys to have a place to run to."

Sasha slowly rose to her feet and made her way to the door, "Thank You."

Chapter Twenty-Two

Sasha stared up at the house as she stepped out of the jeep. Well, *house* was not the right word. Where she was staying for the next few days was a mansion or a manor, she was not sure what to call it. It was at least four stories high with too many windows to count and every couple of windows there was a balcony. Vines climbed the side of the dark brick exterior. All in all, it was beautiful. She walked up the stairs leading to the entrance and took in the large family crest on top of the door. It was a circle that had vines woven around it, with words written in a language that she could barely make out.

The door opened revealing two men in suits. Sasha halted until Cormac walked passed her and shook hands with both men.

They walked into a wide foyer. Two grand staircases wrapped up on opposites sides of the room connecting up to an ornate second-floor balcony.

"Hello!" A loud, boisterous voice greeted them. Brandon Baron, she guessed. He stood on the balcony dressed in an expensive tailored black suit. He was older - looked to be in his mid-seventies, with salt and pepper hair, and tight eyes. Even though he was smiling at them, she could tell he was all business. "I am Brandon Baron and welcome to my home. I'm so delighted to have you all here." He opened his arms wide in what he thought was a welcoming gesture. "Safe and sound thanks to Cormac and Derek. I know you all must be tired from your journey, so I will not keep you long. I would like to give you a quick tour before you retire to your rooms. Cormac, you and your son, will have the same rooms as last time. I do hope you remember where everything is. If you would like to retire to your rooms, you may do so," he instructed. "Everyone else, I will make this tour short for your benefit." Cormac nodded, and he and Derek grabbed their bags and headed up the stairs.

Brandon cleared his throat. "The door to your left is the parlor. It is there for your use, as is the library, which is through the door on your right. Now, if you'll follow me, I will show you the rooms you are allowed to enter. While I am happy to have you, please remember that this is my private home. There will be rooms that are off limits to you all," he said, turning down the hallway. "Leave your bags here; you may grab them on your way back."

The group followed Brandon down the hall. They made a left and continued down another dark hall. It was decorated with small statues and with what Sasha could only guess was expensive art work. Brandon walked halfway down the corridor before he stopped in front of grand double doors and pushed them open.

"This is the dining room. All meals will be served in this room. This includes tonight's dinner, which will be served promptly at 7:00 pm. I expect you all to be in attendance, as I know we will have much to discuss." He closed the doors and walked further down the hall, with everyone following close behind. They walked down the rest of the hallway, passing doors Brandon didn't bother to mention. Sasha assumed those were some of the rooms they were not allowed in. They turned another corner and came to a stop in front of another door, much different from the rest. It was noticeably smaller.

"This leads downstairs to my underground bunker. Down there is the training area, which is available for you to use at your discretion." He said quickly, then turned around and led them back to the front where their bags sat waiting.

"Now, grab your bags and follow me. I'll show you to your rooms, where you will have time to relax before dinner." He headed up the stairs. Sasha noticed that it took considerable effort on Brandon's part but made no mention of it. When they reached the landing, he walked to the right, stopped at the first room and turned to face them.

"Sasha," he said, turning his focus to her. "You and Cassie will be sharing this room; your bath room is connected inside." He opened the door slightly before turning to the door directly across from them. "This room belongs to Danny and Devin; you will find your room has its own bathroom as well. I will let you all get settled. Wendy your room is down the hall. Follow me."

Sasha and Cassie entered their new room and paused at the beauty. There were two full canopy beds, each with long, black curtains surrounding the bed. The beds themselves were made of a dark wood. The bedposts were intricately carved with designs of nature. The walls were dark with an outline of flowers embossed on them. Two armoires matched the beds in color and beauty. Matching night stands sat next to the beds for each of them.

"This room is amazing," Cassie gushed. "I could stay here forever!" She dropped her bags on the floor and jumped on the bed.

"You might have to," Sasha muttered under her breath.

"Oh… And it's *so* comfortable." Cassie moaned ignoring Sasha's comment, as her body became a willing hostage to the bed.

"Really? Is all of that necessary?" Sasha laughed dropping her bags on the floor before lying on her bed. " I retract my last statement," Sasha said, snuggled deeper. "It's like I'm on a cloud!"

"I know right!" Cassie agreed. "I mean, if we have to be on the run, this is a nice place to hide." Cassie sat up on her elbows. "How long until dinner?"

"An hour," Devin said from the doorway, startling both girls.

"Don't do that!" Sasha yelled, tossing a

pillow at him. He caught it and held onto it walking into the room; he flopped on Sasha's bed.

"Hey, this is my bed!" She nudged him with her foot trying to push him off the bed.

"Is this how you treat family!" He rolled on his back pushing her foot away.

"Go share with Cassie." Sasha nudged him again.

"Cassie's off limits," Devin placed the pillow under his head.

"What?" Cassie sat up. "Why am I off limits?"

Devin rolled his eyes at her giving her a knowing look. "Are you going to make me say it?"

"Make you say what?" Cassie asked a bit too innocently.

"Don't act like you don't know." Devin nodded to her.

"Fine." Cassie huffed, but a small smile graced her lips.

"This place is huge." Danny joined them walking over to Cassie's bed, dropping on it.

Sasha bit back a smile when Danny's hand reached out grabbed Cassie's ankle. He pulled her closer and started to play with the hem of her pants.

"Very astute of you my dear brother."
Devin retorted. "So, what do you guys have
planned until dinner?" Devin asked.

Sasha shrugged. "All I have planned is a
hot shower to wash that car ride off me."

"Is Derek going to join you?" Cassie
teased.

"Don't be stupid." Sasha threw a pillow
at her which Danny knocked out of the air.

"Well, I was thinking about checking out
the grounds." Cassie looked to Danny
silently asking him.

"Sounds cool." Danny agreed. "Let's
go." He stood up reaching out a hand to her.

Cassie gave Sasha and Devin a small
wave and placed her hand in his.

"See you two later!" Sasha called after
them. She rolled over to the edge of her bed
letting her feet touch the ground before
standing up. She pulled her bag on top of the
bed and started rummaging for clean
clothes. "How about we meet in the library
in twenty minutes? I want to shower first."

"Fine with me." He stood and rolled his
shoulders. "See you there."

~~

Twenty minutes later, Sasha found
herself in the library. Devin was already

sitting at a table far in the back, with a pile of books surrounding him.

"I see you've been busy…" Sasha dropped in the seat across from him.

"Yeah," he looked up. "This library is either very amazing or incredibly creepy – I still need time to decide." He paused. "Most of these books are all about us." Devin pointed between them. "They are exclusively about our family history, starting from the first king. I've found stuff in here that I have never discovered in any history book."

"Oh," she flipped through pages. "That sounds like creepy to me."

"It is *not* creepy to have this information," Brandon said. He walked out of the book stacks scaring the two teens. "My apologies," he held up his hand in mock surrender,"It was not my intention to startle you both, but I saw the light on and wanted to see if you needed any assistance."

"I hope it's okay for us to be in here. We just wanted to check out the books in your collection, and you did say this room was open to us." Devin stood up.

"No, no, it is quite alright," Brandon said with a wave of his hand. "But to clear up any future confusion. My family has been the official historians for the Royal Family for generations. It has been my family's job to record your family's growth. After I had realized the switch that took place a few years ago, I decided to retire. Now that I am in the presences of the real Royals. I hope all of this hard work will help you learn everything you desire to know about your family. Enjoy the books, but please remember that dinner is in less than an hour. I would appreciate it if you were not late." He walked back into the stacks and out of the room, just as quietly as he came.

"Weird but helpful," Devin admitted once Brandon was out of ear shot.

"What are we waiting for, we only have a few days." Sasha took the book that was closest to her and started on page one.

Chapter Twenty-Three

Sasha and Devin made it into the dining room with five minutes to spare. It seemed like they were the last ones to arrive.

The dining room held a long dark wood dining table that spanned at least ten feet long. Brandon sat at the head of the table. Wendy was to his left, and Cormac sat at his right. Derek was next to his father. Danny and Cassie were next to Wendy, and there were only two open seats left – one right next to Derek.

Sasha took the open seat closest to Derek, ignoring the look Cassie gave her, and Devin sat on her other side.

"Thank you all for being on time." Brandon started once they were seated. "Dinner will be served in a few minutes."

"You said we have a lot to discuss," Wendy said cutting to the point.

"Yes," Brandon nodded.

"I want to know what will happen to Cassie once we leave?" Wendy asked.

Sasha took a quick glance at Cassie, Danny had his arm slung over the back of Cassie's chair.

"I spoke to your parents after you arrived," he nodded to Cassie. "We have agreed that Cassie should stay for the next few weeks. Then she will be found wandering in the woods a few miles outside of town."

"How are you going to pull that off in a believable manner?" Wendy pushed. "People are going to expect a battered and bruised starving girl."

"We spoke about that as well." Brandon kept on. "I am sorry to say Cassie that for the next few weeks before you are found, we will have to cut back on the food you are given and the type. We need to make it look like you were only given the bare minimum to survive."

"So she will lose a considerable amount of weight. What else?" Wendy pressed on.

"The story that we are going to go with is they were held in an unknown location away from Jasmine. The girls tried to escape but Sasha was killed, and Cassie ran for her

life. Thus it will end the search for Sasha
and explain why she only has a few days of
exposure. We have a power blocking
necklace that you will wear only the day of."
He assured. "Also every day for a couple of
hours a day and while you sleep. You
will start wearing bindings on your wrist and
ankles so that you will have the marks on
your skin, and they will start looking healed
over when you are found. I know it sounds
like a lot but for the public and the Enforcers
to believe the story you need to have all the
marks." His eyes drilled into Cassie.

"I can handle it," Cassie assured as she
looked at Sasha.

"Are you sure?" Sasha asked.

"I can do it." Cassie re-assured. "It won't
be fun, but I'll do it to keep you safe."

"The other question I have," Wendy
spoke up again. "They will know this story
is fake. Do you think they will come after
her?"

Brandon shook his head. "Cassie being
found will be national news, her story will
be on every newspaper's front page. While
those behind this will know the story is fake,
it will be in their best interest not to
comment on it. Cassie's story will throw the

scent off of them. She will say it was someone from Jasmine's past. The attackers wanted information about one of their past crimes that she supposedly was a part of then ended up turning on them."

"So we dirty up my mother's name more?" Sasha felt heat grow in her chest.

"Sasha, we need a story that will please the public, and ease the fears of everyone behind it."

"Then why not just tell the truth!" Sasha exclaimed. "When Cassie is found she can just say it was the crown who attacked us."

"Then they would brand her as part of your mother's conspiracy," Brandon explained. "What they've already released about Jasmine has already ruined her name in the eyes of the public. If we do it your way, Cassie's name will go down just like hers and what is worse." He took a breath. "They will know she knows the truth and then who knows what they will do. They could brand her a traitor and throw her in jail. If we go with the plan her parents and I discussed, she will most likely be watched for the rest of her life, but she will be safe."

"Being watched for the rest of my life," Cassie spoke up. "But then...I'll never be able to come see you guys again." Danny's arm dropped around her shoulder giving it a squeeze.

"No, it will never be safe, you will need to live your life with the belief you are always being watched," Brandon said.

The door opened, and a few maids entered each carrying two plates. One by one they placed plates in front of each guest.

"Enjoy," Brandon ordered once the last plate touched the table.

Chapter Twenty-Four

Sasha strolled down the aisle of the massive library; books were her secret love. Not that she told many people. She loved the smell of old books; the musty, dusty smell always seemed to calm her in a way that she couldn't explain.

This library was better than the one back home... minus all the book about her family. She found a chair deep in the back, took her seat, and pulled out the journal she brought with her from Wendy's.

She turned to where she left off last.

For a while I just watched her. I needed proof that I could take to my father to prove the woman he married had deceived him. But no such luck. She was good; I had to give her that, My guard John agreed with me. He knew there was something off about Victoria but alas like me he could not prove it.

So we just watched, and he would report back to me. We acted like this for two long

years until she announced she was pregnant.
*I was sure **it** did not belong to my father*
because she was far too friendly with one of
her guards. Much more than a married
Queen ought to be.

But my ever blinded father did not see
what was transpiring right under his nose.
He was blinded by the happiness of having
another child. Something my mother could
never give him after me. He started to dote
on her more and more, and I could see she
was not as happy to have him around her so
much. I could see she longed to be in the
arms of another. The arms of her guard.

But proof? That is what John said we
needed before we voiced our concerns. If we
would accuse without proof, she could get
away. Then what would happen when we
finally had the proof? No one would believe
us....he did not want me to be the boy who
cried wolf. I respected him... so I held my
tongue. Now I wish I had not and instead
shouted to the high heavens what I knew to
be true. Proof be damned.

When she finally gave birth to her
spawn... my father threw a party. Once
again those he deemed important enough
came to view the new prince.

When it was my turn to hold him, I fought very hard not to drop him on the stone floor. It was not his fault he was born into this mess...to that woman. He should not be punished for his parent's mistakes.

I looked around the room that day...everyone in the room were people who wanted to be seen by my father and myself. People who were ready to do anything to get in our good graces. I shook my head in disgust at the thought. I know it's a morbid thought to view people this way, but growing up royal you learn to see the true intentions of those around you. My mother made sure she raised me to always see people for who they are. She wanted to make sure people would never be able to advantage of me. Not so I never trusted anyone, but I would be able to see who really cared. The people in that room did not truly care about us... they cared about power.

I remember Victoria pushing me to hold him often. He was a pretty baby, but he favored Victoria. At least she would not have to explain why my 'brother' favored another man. Why could he not look like his true father... then my father would see the truth....she could have never hidden that.

Whenever she said the word 'brother,'
she had the smug look about her. Like she
was goading me ... telling me with the word
'brother' she had won ... what she won I was
not sure at the time. Having this boy did not
change anything in the long run. I was still
first in line. I would be Queen, I would rule.
I wish I knew then what I know now. I would
have acted faster instead of biding my time.

There was a moment that I thought I had
acted fast enough. I was in the garden
talking to my mother ... I needed her
guidance when I overheard voices speaking
... Victoria's voice.

She was in the garden in the dead of
night talking to one of my father's servants.
He was new ... only worked at the castle for a
few months. I made a point to notice who
came in my father's presence ever since she
caught his eye.

From where I was sitting they couldn't
see me, but I could hear them. Not as well as
I would have liked but well enough to
understand they were plotting against my
father. I could only make out bits and
pieces of their conversation ... but enough to
understand I needed to warn my father.

I ran to my guard John and told him at

once what I heard. He went into action to find the servant, but in the thirty minutes it took me to find John... the servant disappeared.

It made no sense. No one could find him, and once again my father said I was over reacting. That I was still dealing with the grief of losing my mother and I was not thinking or seeing clearly.

I wish I could say I walked away after he spoke those words to me, but alas I did not. We argued...and argued... and argued. All the pent up frustration I had... the anger and distrust I had over Victoria came out tenfold. I spoke words to my father that I wish I could take back... words I would never be able to say sorry for.

That night I went to bed angrier than I ever thought possible. It was John who woke me that night, and I'll never forget the look on his face when he came into my room. I knew just by looking at him my father was dead. Before I could act another guard came in and he rushed me out of my room through a secret panel, I did not know existed. They snuck me out of the castle.

I didn't want to leave. It made me look like I had something to do with my father's death. I tried to explain, but Vincent, my father's guard, told me Victoria had already placed the blame on me. The last words I spoke to my father were 'You are dead to me...I wish you had died and not mother'. I cannot tell you how much I wish I could take those words back.

The argument I had with my father was viewed by many people. There were witnesses that heard me say I hated him.

I told Vincent that I should still go back and explain my side. My words were that of an angry teen, and I did not mean it. I had no reason to take my father's life, and an argument is not proof of my guilt.

He told me it was all the proof they needed, and he told me what was kept from me. Victoria was trying to take the crown from me. For weeks she was whispering in my father's ear. Trying to get him to change his mind and give the crown to 'their son,' that all the Rulers beforehand had been male.

I pointed out that was because they were the firstborn not because they were male. He explained to me that it did not matter. Certain people in the kingdom did not want a woman to rule and that my father

was slowly seeing their side. I was
heartbroken at the thought that my father
would even think to take their side.
  So I listened, and I followed after him
and together in the dead of night while the
castle searched for me, I ran.
  "Sasha, what are you doing up?"
  Sasha jumped in her seat. "What the..."
she looked up and saw Derek staring at her.
"Don't do that!" she screamed at him.
  "Sorry!" he held up his hands in mock
surrender. "I didn't mean to scare you."
  "What are you doing in here?" she
closed the journal.
  "I couldn't sleep so I figured I would
wander around. I saw a light on in here." He
explained looking her up and down
reminding Sasha she was only in a pair of
shorts and a tank top. It was her normal
sleep attire but, around him, she wished she
was wearing something a bit nicer.
  "Sure…" she stood, "Well I'm going to
go," she started past him.
  "Wait..." he called after her. "What are
you reading?" he pointed to the journal
tucked under her arm.
  "Nothing. Really. Just a journal." She
held it behind her a bit. "But I should be

going... early training session in the morning with your Dad," she started to turn.

"Let me walk you up." He offered to come and started to fall into step next to her. "No... it's ok." She assured. "I'll be fine." She said once they made it to the steps. She started up them hoping he stayed away, getting attached to anyone new was not a smart idea right now.

Thankfully, he didn't follow her. She walked the hall to her room wishing she didn't regret him not walking her.... Why did he have to be so cute....?

Chapter Twenty-Five

Sasha walked down the long hallway, on her way to her first training session with Cormac and Wendy. Wendy wanted to sit in for this training session. She wanted to observe Cormac's training techniques and see if she could learn anything that could help Sasha down the road.

Sasha finally found the door Brandon showed them and headed downstairs. She looked up and down the hall looking for the door labeled *Training Room*.

"Hey, Sasha." Derek greeted her as he walked out of the room.

"Hey... Derek." Sasha paused, taking in his form. He was wearing loose dark shorts and a fitted sleeveless shirt that clung to his sweaty body. His breath was slightly ragged, his hair was matted to his forehead, and his body glowed with a fine sheen of sweat. There was a slight magnetic hum that surrounded him and called to her in a way she did not understand, nor did she want to.

Derek ran his hand through his messy hair and smiled causing butterflies to erupt in her stomach. "On your way to train?" he asked.

Sasha nodded, "Yeah, with Wendy and your Dad." She walked around him and reached for the door.

"Hey, I've been meaning to ask you," Derek moved in front of her, blocking her entrance to the training room. "How are you handling everything?"

"Um, pretty well I guess since you know I will never see my mother again." She shifted her weight from one foot to another.

"Dumb question." Derek gave her a nervous laugh. "Sorry."

"No, it's OK." She waved it off. "Thanks for asking though."

"You're welcome...but um," he paused trying to find his words. "You know if you ever want to talk about it while you are here, I'm available."

"Umm... Thanks, but no thanks." She saw his smile drop as his demeanor change. "Nothing personal," she rushed out, trying to save the conversation. "It's just that...well, right now I have Cassie, you know, girl talk and all." She pointed out. "Plus, she is already up to speed and knows how I think." She tucked a piece of hair behind her ear. "So she qualified for the job." She gave him a nervous laugh.

Derek nodded slowly. "Well, have a good day training, and don't let my father go too hard on you," he waved and headed for the stairs.

Sasha waved back before she took a deep breath and opened the door. Just like the rest of the house, the training room was state of the art. There was an open mat in the middle of the room where Cormac and Wendy were standing. Around the room, there were multiple workout machines. There was a treadmill, stair climber, and free weights stacked against one wall in front of a large mirror. It was evident that Brandon had put a lot of effort into this room.

"Sasha, there you are!" Cormac greeted finally noticed her arrival. "Let's get started. Today all we want to focus on is your shield strength." Cormac brought a few rubber balls in the air and let them rotate around him.

Sasha nodded and focused on what she had already learned. A wall of glass protecting her.

"Do you have it?" Wendy asked.

Sasha nodded and prepared for Cormac's attack. She hissed as a ball broke through her shield and slammed into her leg. She would have a bruise later. She rubbed the impact spot and looked down; there was a small rubber ball lying next to her foot.

"You were not prepared," Wendy stated from behind her.

"But I wasn't expecting you to attack." Sasha turned to her.

"You never know who is a danger to you Sasha. When you make a shield, always protect your back." Wendy explained.

"Now let's try again." Cormac and Wendy lifted their objects in the air once more. Sasha nodded and formed her shield around her body.

Chapter Twenty-Six

Sasha rolled her shoulders as she headed into the library. Cassie mentioned she was going to be there most of the morning with Danny and Devin reading up about the family. Plus, it was one of the times that she needed to wear the bindings. She didn't want to be trapped in the room while she was tied up.

"You look like crap," Danny commented seeing Sasha's bruised body.

"Well, I feel worse." She sighed as she slid down into the seat.

"Did it not go well?" Cassie asked.

Sasha shook her head. "It went pretty good. We worked on shields today. As you can tell." She gestured to her body. "It took me a bit to build one strong enough to keep out full strength attacks."

"But you were able to?" Devin asked.

"Yea." Sasha nodded with a smile. "After I took way too many hits from your Mom."

"That's great!" Cassie tried to clap her bound hands but found it was a bit more difficult than she thought it would be.

"How's that going?" Sasha motioned to Cassie's wrists.

"Ehh," she shrugged. "Not great, they are so annoying, and they keep pinching my skin."

"That's why you have them on," Devin said flipping his book closed and opening another one.

"Thank you, Captain Obvious." Cassie rolled her eyes. "I was there when they explained it; I even made them tie them tighter for a better mark."

"Just saying," Devin said flipping through the book.

"What are you looking for?" Sasha asked Devin.

"Nothing really just trying to read everything I can." He turned the page.

"You can't read that fast, can you?" she asked as he skimmed down the page and turned to another.

"Oh, we never did tell you. We have eidetic memories, so yes, we can read that fast."

"Except I use mine." Devin shot a look

at his brother.

"I like to save mine for something more important." Danny looked at Cassie and tucked a strand behind her ear.

"And on that note!" Sasha stood stretching her sore muscles. "I am going to take a bath and hope my body starts to feel better." She rolled her shoulders and walked in the door. "See you guys at lunch!" She called closing the door behind her.

Sasha hummed to herself as she walked to her room. She thought about how great the bath was going to feel as she pushed into her room. She pulled off her shoes and flopped on her bed. "*Maybe a nap before the bath,*" she thought as she snuggled deeper into the bed.

She flopped on her back and reached over and grabbed a book from her night table. She would read until she fell asleep.

"What are you reading?" Derek asked as he walked into her bedroom. She dropped the book and turned to the door.

"Why does no one knock in this place?" She sat up. "You know this is a girl's room – I could have been changing."

"That's a risk I am willing to take," he said, wiggling his eyebrows at her. "But I digress. So, I ask again, what are you reading?" He asked as he shut the door behind him.

"Nothing. Just a book on Gabriela that I got from down stairs. I wanted to learn more about her since all I was taught was that she was a traitor."

Derek came closer to the bed and glanced at the opened page, "You know you look like her," he commented, and Sasha scoffed.

"What are you talking about? I do not."

Derek sat on the edge of her bed and pulled the book into his lap.

"Hey!" Sasha protested. "I was about to read that." She reached for the book.

"I'm not keeping it," Derek answered, shoving her hand away. "I just wanted to see another photo of her." He flipped through the book. "Here," he said, showing her a full portrait of Gabriela. "There aren't many pictures of her left. It was said Victoria had them all destroyed after Gabriela's betrayal. But in this photo, you two could be sisters." He showed her the photo.

Sasha took a glance at the photo before shaking her head, "I don't see it."

Derek shook his head as he started

pointing at the features, "You two have the same eyes, same nose, and the same bone structure. Yeah, the hair is different and so is the mouth, but you two look a lot alike."

"If you say so," Sasha waved him off, "Anyway, why are you here?"

"I wanted to see how your training went," he shrugged. "And I saw the door open, so I figured I would see what you were up to."

Sasha gave him a blank stare. "Really?"

"I know, but I figured I would ask. Do you want to talk about it?" Derek leaned back on her bed, making himself comfortable.

"I really have nothing to talk about. Every decision has been made for me. I just want to train and hang out with Cassie while I can."

"Understandable." He nodded.

"Are you going to tell me why you are really here?"

"I told you, I just wanted to see…how your first day went?"

"You could have done that at lunch."

"Fine you caught me," he sat up. "I wanted to see you."

"Why?"

He shrugged. "You're cute."

Sasha rolled her eyes. "Nice line."

"Just stating a fact." He winked at her.

"Ok, Mr. Smooth," she stood up ignoring the flutters in the lower belly. "I need to take a bath then a nap before lunch is served."

"Meet me in the maze after lunch." Derek stood up.

"Why?"

"Just meet me," he opened the door, "and come alone." He winked and shut the door behind him.

Sasha waited until she heard his footsteps head away from her door before walking into the bathroom.

Chapter Twenty-Seven

Jasmine sat in her cell; feeling her body grow weaker with every passing minute. She had no idea why they were keeping her alive. It made no sense. They had to know she would never tell them where her daughter was. No matter what they put her through, and they had put her through a lot. She would never put what was left of her family in danger. Not again.

She rolled over in her cell and hugged her knees to her chest.

"Hello, Jasmine."

The familiar voice sent chills running down her body. "Hello, Alex," she whispered, turning to face him. "Time for another visit already?"

"This could be simple for you. Just give us the answers we are looking for, and you could have a quick and simple death, eventually." he taunted. *Finally, after all this time, she was returned to him.*

"Go to hell, Alex," she spat out blood on the cold stone floor. "I will never tell you."

"Don't you want to join your husband?" he sneered, glaring down at her with a look of pure hatred.

"Yes, I would love to be with the love of my life," Jasmine sneered. "Why don't you send me?"

He growled at her words. "We're not done yet." He paced in front of her cell. "You know, I've watched you for years." He admitted.

"Then why have you waited so long to come after me?" Jasmine asked. "You always did like to play with your food before you ate it." She commented as an afterthought.

"I said I knew where you were. My parents, however, had no idea until recently. Naturally, they are upset with me for hiding your location, and who could blame them? I had to explain that I was having you watched so you would lead me to your sister's location. It appeased them." Alex walked up to the cell and whispered, "But we know that's not true, don't we Jasmine? I just enjoyed knowing your life was in my hands and having the option of ending it whenever I wanted to. I love having that power over you, and while you are here, I still do." He grinned down at her. "Now I am going to make you pay, every day, for what you put me through."

"You're a monster," she said, refusing to look at him.

"And who made me this way?" he roared, causing her to jump. "You did! I loved you Jasmine and what did you do? You betrayed me! Even after I learned who you really were, I offered to let you live and still, you left me. You went and married some other man, not even a month after you left me! And then you spawned that bastard's child. If you think I'm monster, you have only yourself to blame. This is your fault."

"No!" she screamed, standing up carefully. She forced her weak body over to the prison bars that stood between them. But she was careful not to touch them. "You made yourself this way. I had nothing to do with it. You never loved me, Alex. If you had, you would have stood up to your parents for me. Everything I did, I did for my family. Your parents killed my parents…my aunt…my grandparents. They took everything from me. They didn't want to rule. They just wanted to live out in the open." She took a breath. "Your family wanted my family dead, and I was just supposed to be okay with that." She shook her head. "I won't apologize for wanting justice for my family." She glared at him. It felt good after all those years to stand up to him and put him in his place.

Alex glared at her and reached through the cell, grabbing her by the neck before she could react. He pulled her to the bars, relishing her whimpers of pain as the bars burned her skin. She clawed at his hand trying to free her airway.

"I'm going to find your daughter," he hissed, pulling her closer and increasing his grip. "And I am going to keep you alive until I do. Then, when you are too weak to help or even to cry out for mercy. I am going to put her in the cell next to yours and have every horrible act you can think of carried out. You will hear every scream and every cry for help. You will listen to every plea for mercy; knowing there is nothing you can do. She will cry out for you, and you will come. When I know that I have broken her will to live and my men have had their fill of her body. When she is begging for death, only then will I grant it. It will be a slow and painful and I will make you watch every second of it. Then and only then, when I know I have completely broken you, I will grant you death in the same manner as your precious daughter." He threw her on the stone floor as hard as he could. She gasped in pain as her head bounced on the stone floor.

She looked up at him and felt the room spinning; her sight started to fade. She drew in a shaky breath as she felt the waiting arms of unconsciousness start to wrap around her. "She's," she struggled to speak. "She's yours…" she whispered and fell into the darkness' sweet embrace.

She never saw his eyes widen. She never heard him scream at her to wake up. She never heard him beg to know if she was telling the truth.

Chapter Twenty-Eight

"So I'm here," Sasha said, once she spotted Derek sitting on the bench. "The question is why?"

"I want to help you." He stood up.

"Help me how?"

"With your training." He stated as if it was obvious.

"I thought your father was helping me with that?"

"Yeah, he is." Derek nodded.

"Well, what do you want to help me with?"

"Hand to hand combat," Derek said as he closed the distance between them.

"But I have powers now," Sasha said, confused.

"Hand to hand combat is still an important skill to have."

"What do you think you can teach me?" she raised an eyebrow to him.

Derek didn't answer. Instead, he dropped to the ground stuck his leg out and swept it under Sasha legs knocking her to the ground.

"Ow!" Sasha groaned as she landed on her butt. "What was that for?"

"That's how I can help you." He reached out a hand and helped her to her feet. "If you want to stay hidden, you won't always be able to use your powers. I want to make sure you can defend yourself."

"No more cheap shots?" She asked dusting off her shorts.

"Promise." He winked.

She rolled her eyes. "Ok fine, then I agree. But why are we meeting out here and not in the training room?"

"I thought we could keep this between you and me."

"Any particular reason why?"

"No, I just like having a secret with you." He smiled.

"Yeah like I believe that, but I won't push it for now."

"Good, because I have a lot to teach you and not a lot of time to do it, so let's get started."

"Teach away!" She waved her hand in front of her.

"Get into your fighting stance." He

ordered, and Sasha adjusted her stance. "Ok not bad." He circled around her and Sasha felt his eyes linger more on her curves than on her stance.

"We only need to fix a few things." He reached out and adjusted her body – squaring her hips, adjusting her shoulders, and widening her stance.

She stiffened when she felt his hand glide along her waist. Skimming right under her shirt touching her skin longer than needed.

"Sorry," he pulled as he noticed the change in her body.

"It's ok." She whispered ignoring the heat between them.

He stood in front of her and held his hand up. "Hit me."

"What?" Her stance faltered a bit.

"Hit me!" He repeated, "I want to see how you look throwing a punch."

Sasha punched with her right fist aiming for his head. Her hand reached out and blocked her.

"Not bad, do it again."

She led with her left fist, but he blocked it again. She threw punch after punch for the next couple of minutes, but Derek blocked them all.

"This is pointless, I'm not going to hit you," Sasha complained dropping her arms.

"That's not the point of this lesson. I want to see what I am working with to know the best way to train you." He explained, stepping aside. "Now keep going. Just punch the air. I want to see from a different angle."

Sasha nodded and started again. She could see out of the corner of her eyes Derek walking around her but she kept focused on her task.

"Now kick." He commanded.

Sasha hesitated but lifted her leg and kicked in the way she saw on television.

"Ok, stop." He said. "You are not as bad as I thought."

"Gee thanks." She deadpanned.

"Watch me." He said getting into a fighting stance. "The way you are punching you are throwing your shoulder into it and, as a result, you are throwing your body out of balance. Watch." He threw a couple of punches, mimicking Sasha's form. "Keep your shoulders square when you punch. Like this." He threw a couple more punches with the corrected form. "Try it."

Sasha nodded and got back to the stance she was in before, and mimicked his movement.

"Good. Now when you kick, you want to shift your body to make sure you don't lose your balance. When you kicked before I saw your body wobble a bit." He demonstrated a kick. "You got it?" Sasha nodded. "Try it."

Sasha once again mimicked his form.

"Better but you are still wobbling a bit. Kick again but leave your leg up."

Sasha kicked and held her leg in the air once it was fully extended.

"Here," he grabbed her leg, turned it slightly and then lowered it, "Don't kick too high. That throws off your center of gravity, and you can tip backward before the kick lands." He grabbed her shoulders and lifted her slightly. "You don't want to lean too far back either." His breath brushed across her neck, and she felt the heat rise and flood her cheeks. "Understand?"

She nodded not trusting her voice.

"Good, you can lower your leg now."

Sasha lowered her leg but stayed in fighting stance.

Derek positioned himself in front of Sasha. "Try and hit me again."

Sasha led with her right, but he blocked it. "Better. Now when you lead with your right, I want you to cross with your left like this." He showed her.

Sasha nodded and tried it again. "Good," he said catching her fist in his hand. "Make sure you keep your fist in line with your wrist. Too high or too low and you can really injure your hand." He explained his hand sliding up her arm. Sasha felt goose bumps form on her skin in the wake of his hand. "Your power comes from here." He rubbed her arm.

Sasha nodded, but her attention was not on what he was saying, but on him and the way he was looking at her. She felt him lower her arm and she turned to face him. His gaze was intense like he was staring into her soul. She turned her head trying to look away, but his hand shot up and grabbed her chin forcing her to look at him. She saw him glance at her lips then back at her eyes almost if he was asking permission. Sasha felt herself nod, and he started to lean in.

"So this is why you came to the maze?" Devin's voice snapped the two out of their bubble. Derek took a step back from Sasha, who self-consciously ran her hand through her hair.

"Devin! What are you doing here?" Sasha looked at her amused cousin.

"Cassie wants to speak to you. She's a bit tied up at the moment, and I told her I would come and find you." Devin looked between them. "Though I feel like this is a situation she would love to see," he smirked.

Sasha rolled her eyes at her cousin. "We were just talking."

"Sure... It seems I have been *talking* to girls all wrong." Devin laughed, and he escorted Sasha out of the maze. Derek watched them go as a look of annoyance crossed his face.

Chapter Twenty-Nine

"You were about to kiss him!" Cassie
leaned forward on the bed.

"I was not!"

"Yes you were, remember eidetic
memory I know what I saw." Devin teased.

"Ugh!" Sasha leaned back on her bed.

"Are you ready to admit you like him?"

"No! Because an attraction does not
mean affection." Sasha defended.

"Devin, why did you interrupt them?"
Cassie scolded. "You should have waited
until they kissed. Now he might not ever
make another move on her again, and then
Sasha could not keep lying to herself."

"It's not like I want him to try again!"

"Stop lying!" Cassie accused. "You want
him to try again, and I want that for you. We
need to make sure you are alone with him
again."

"What? No!" Sasha said as she shook her
head. "Why would you?"

"Ok bringing up the elephant in the

room!" Cassie winced as her shift in weight pulled on the ties too tightly. "You have like three and a half more days left of being a semi-normal teenager in this situation. This is your last chance at a teenage romance with someone who knows the truth. Enjoy it. That's what Danny and I are doing." She leaned over to him. Danny wrapped his arm around her shoulder and kissed her forehead. "It sucks to know in a few days I will never see him again. But we are not going to let that stop our feelings, and you should not let this stop you."

"Seriously why couldn't Brandon have a cute granddaughter here? I want to have a teenage romance." Devin grumbled from his spot on Sasha's bed earning a laugh from the room.

"Well anyway, you didn't want to talk to me about Derek when Devin came looking for me. What did you want to talk to me about?"

"Changing the subject, fine I will let you do it for now." Cassie conceded. "Brandon gave me a phone I talked to my parents, and they told me something that I need to tell you."

"What?" Sasha asked,

"Well, we haven't been following the news, so we didn't know. But Susan, she was killed."

"What?" Sasha felt her stomach drop. "How?"

"My parents didn't tell me. But they said it's connected to what happened to us; they think the same people who attacked us went after her. She was the first person on the scene. The running theory in town is everyone thinks Susan might have seen the men who attacked us. But that's not the big thing?" Cassie paused. "They told me that Susan had a hidden laptop that she used to send reports."

"What type of reports?" Sasha was almost too scared to ask.

"Reports on you and your mom." She explained. "She was sending them to someone, but they're not sure who."

"She was spying on us?" Sasha couldn't believe what her best friend was telling her. "But she was Mom's best friend."

"They think she was planted in your lives like they did with me." Cassie's voice trailed off at the end.

Sasha took a moment to process everything she just heard. "How did they find out? I doubt the news reported all of that?"

"No, um my parents' friend George told them. They said he's part of the group as well. He wanted to know if they knew anything about the laptop."

"Enforcer George is a part of this?"

"Seems so."

"Do they have any idea why she was spying on us? Who she was sending it to?"

Cassie shook her head. "No, but Enforcer George thinks it might have been someone at the castle."

"What?! That doesn't make any sense. The crown wants us dead."

"I know, that's what I said. But they think someone inside the castle wanted to know how you were doing at all times."

Chapter Thirty

"Robert I need to talk to you," Kaitlin said rushing into his office shutting the door behind her. "I was doing a bit more searching into the clone laptop I read and re-read one of her files, and I saw something weird. I checked it out, and one thing leads to another, and I found something." She placed her laptop on his desk. "I found this." She pulled up a blank page.

"It's blank Kaitlin," Robert said.

"No." Kaitlin smiled. "It only looks blank, but the file is too big to be blank. There is a message on this page."

"I take it by the way you are smiling; you know what the message is." He looked up at her.

"Yep." She nodded. She turned the laptop around, tapped on a couple of keys, and turned it back around. Robert watched as letters started to form on the page as if he was typing.

"We need to see the Lightworths and

George now." He stood up and headed for the door. Kaitlin grabbed the laptop and followed after him.

The drive to the Lightworth's house was a quick but quiet one. Kaitlin could feel the anger rolling off him in waves. She knew he was going to be upset with what she found, but she also knew there was no way she could keep this information from him.

They arrived as George was pulling up as well. He was supporting a look of confusion as to why they were all there. Kaitlin was sure that look would be gone within five minutes of Robert's speech.

Cathy opened the door before Robert could knock.

"Enforcer Robert, Kaitlin, George, is everything ok with the case? Did you find out anything new?" She asked as they all walked into the living room. She sat down next to her husband, Kaitlin and George sat down across from them while Robert paced the room.

"You know, I was about to ask you the same question." He shook his head turning to Cathy and John.

John and Cathy shared a confused look, but it was John who spoke up, "What are you talking about Robert?"

Robert snorted. "You can drop the act."

George stood. "Rob, what's going on?"

"George, don't act innocent." Robert turned to him. "Kaitlin and I know the truth. She found the truth."

"What truth?" Cathy asked.

Robert looked to Kaitlin, and she pulled out the laptop. With a few keystrokes, she had the blank page up once more. "I was digging through the laptop from Susan's house. One thing led to another, and I found this." She typed a few more keystrokes and turned the laptop around to face the room.

"You found another report?" George asked.

"I found a report... Just not from Susan." She explained as they got a closer look. George was the first to understand what they were reading.

"Rob..." He started but was quickly cut off.

"Are they even missing?" Robert asked. "We're they even attacked? Should we even care if they are alive?"

"It's not like that," Cathy replied. "We should explain."

"Please do, because from where I am

standing, it's not looking good for any of you."

The three shared a look, but it was George who opened his mouth. "My great-grandfather used to be a guard at the castle. His job was to protect Princess Gabriella."

"The princess who killed her father for the crown?" Kaitlin asked.

"Yes," Cathy picked up the story. "Only it didn't go down the way history remembers. Very few people know the truth, but we know."

"And that would be?" Robert pressed.

"She didn't do it," Cathy said. "She was framed, by her stepmother. What people don't know is while she was in hiding she got married. She had two children. Since then it's been our families' job to protect them."

"You're related?" He pointed between them.

"No, but we've all had a family member who worked at the castle during that time. Each one knew the truth. Each one wanted to protect her family."

"Ok...so what does that story have to do with Jasmine?" Robert asked.

"She's Gabriela's great-granddaughter,"

John answered.

"Wait…" Kaitlin shook her head. "Are you saying what I think you are?"

Cathy nodded. "Yes, they're royalty."

"Even if they are or not that does not explain why they were attacked." Robert cut in.

"It actually does," Cathy said. "Gabriela was framed, for the murder of her father by her stepmother."

"Why is that?" Robert asked.

"The son she gave birth to, wasn't the king's child, but the son of her lover. She needed the king and the princess out of the way so her son could rule." Cathy continued.

"Her son, King Gabriel? King Demenico's father was not the son of King Francis?" Kaitlin pushed.

"No," Cathy said. "When they found Gabriella they didn't know she had a family. They thought they had killed the last of the true royal family. Years ago, Jasmine went to work at the castle to try and find proof of what happened. Somehow she was caught, and her parents and family paid the price. Her sister survived…"

"You know where they are." He cut her

off. "You've known this entire time?"

"Not the entire time," Cathy assured. "We have other contacts around the nation. They found them, and they are with them now. But it was the crown who took Jasmine." Cathy said.

"You've known this entire time?" Robert continued.

"Not the entire time." John clarified. "When you called us we had no idea what had happened. We didn't know she was safe until a few days ago. But with Hunter in town reporting to the crown, we couldn't risk telling anyone."

"Why not bring her back?" Kaitlin asked.

"We can't risk it," Cathy explained.

"The crown wants anyone from Gabriela's line dead. They have the true birth right to the throne." George explained. "Our best guess is that they would assume Cassie knows the truth. Bringing her back wouldn't be safe right now."

"So what the plan?" Robert took a seat.

Cathy started to answer, but a knock on the door distracted them.

Chapter Thirty-One

Sasha groaned as she rolled over in her bed, her body sore from today's latest workout. In the past week at Brandon's house, she had seen tremendous progress. She would train with Cormac in the morning and Derek at night. But all the training came at a cost; she was utterly exhausted. And it seemed like tonight she would not be able to find rest. No position was comfortable enough... Her muscles were just restless. She stood, biting back a hiss as her feet touched the cold floor.

Careful not to wake Cassie, she crept out of the room. Maybe a cup of hot tea would calm her down enough to sleep. She silently hummed to herself as she walked down to the kitchen. She hoped she was allowed back there. In her entire time at the house, they were never allowed behind the scenes as she liked to put it. It was weird to her to be waited on hand and foot by his staff. She was used to doing everything for herself. Her Mom made sure to instill that in her. She walked into the dining room. The maids came from behind that door. She thought that maybe she could get to the kitchen that way.

"Sasha!" She whipped around to see Derek running into the room after her.

"Hey," she smiled, happy to see it was him and not one of Brandon's servants. She didn't want to get in trouble for being where she shouldn't. "What are you doing up?" she asked.

"What are you doing down here?" He ran to her pushing her into a corner away from the windows.

"What's wrong?" She asked, looking up at him confused by his actions.

"You shouldn't be down here..." He looked over his shoulder at the door.

"What why?" she asked. "I just wanted to make a cup of tea to help me sleep. I know that Brandon doesn't like us to go back there, but I didn't want to wake a maid for this. I'm sure he will understand."

"No, you don't understand." He crossed the room, keeping his grip on her arm and checked out the window.

"Derek, what's going on?" She sneaked a peek out the window and froze. Dread filled her body. There were at least six armed men walking the grounds. Each dressed in black, each reminded her of the men who attacked her home. The men who started this mess she was in. "Derek..." She looked up at him.

"Shh!"

She tried to pull her arm back. "We need to warn everyone!"

Derek tightens his grip. "No...you can't."

"Why?" she asked looking up at him.

He shut his eyes trying to come up with an answer. "You weren't supposed to be down here." He cursed under his breath.

"No..." She shook her head in disbelief, his grip on her arm went slack. She backed away from him. "Why? How could you!"

"Keep your voice down." He hissed looking back at the door.

"Why so they don't hear me?! So they don't know I'm ready for them."

"Yes... I need you to be quiet, so I can figure out a new plan for us."

"For us?"

"Yes, you were supposed to stay in your

room." He sighed. "They're already in the house I can't sneak you out this way." He reached out to her.

She shrank back from him. "Why are you doing this?"

"I didn't have a choice." He dropped his hand. "My father planned it."

"And you knew this entire time? Why didn't you tell anyone? Why didn't you warn us?"

"It's complicated." He tried to explain.

"Then un-complicated it." She growled at him; she felt her powers coming alive inside her, bubbling just below the surface of her skin.

"Sasha we don't have time for this. I need to get you out of here. To the maze." He reached for her hand again, but she moved it out of his reach. "Sasha please, I can't let them find you."

"How could you do this to us? Cassie trusted you, her parents trusted you. They got Wendy to trust you and your father, and you abused it!"

"It wasn't my choice; my father did all this, and I just went along with it."

"Did he help plan the attack at my house?" She looked to him for confirmation;

he avoided her eyes giving her, the answer. "How could you!" she slapped him.

"Sasha, please that was before I knew you."

"And that's supposed to make it better?" She scoffed. "My mom could be dead for all I know, and it's your fault!" She felt a jolt of power leave her and hit him directly in his chest.

He recoiled from the blow and caught his breath before speaking. "My dad did this, not me."

"Same thing! You knew what he was going to do and did nothing to stop it. You are just as guilty as he is. I can't believe this."

"Sasha, please you have to trust me. I never planned on letting them get you here; I have a way for us to escape."

"Trust you? Are you out of your mind? In what world, could I ever trust you again? Derek, you've lied to me from the very beginning."

"Please don't say that. Sasha please," he reached for her again.

"I have to warn everyone... while I still can." She made for the door, but Derek blocked her. "Get out of my way before I make you."

"The crown needs someone. Otherwise, they will never stop looking for you... I can only save you... the others not so much."

"Well, that's not good enough for me." She shook her head.

"Sasha..."

"Stay away from me," she glared at him, "I need to get my family out of here."

"You won't be able to get out of here without me... I know their plan."

Sasha shook her head, "Like I could ever trust anything you tell me."

"I was never going to let them take you."

Sasha shook her head and pushed past him. "I don't believe you." She crossed the room back to the window and peeked out again. "How many men??

"At least fifteen, they wanted to make sure no one escaped this time. They are in the house; you will never get to them in time."

"Then you will just have to help me."

"I can help you escape."

"I will not leave my family behind. I won't betray them, I'm not you." she spat at him.

He swallowed thickly, "You can get out through the maze."

"Why should I believe you?"

"I would never hurt you, Sasha," he walked closer to her.

"Stay away from me." She back away from him. "You've hurt me enough already."

He dropped his head. "Just get to the maze, where I trained you." He walked to the wall and opened a panel she did not know was there. He typed in a few numbers, and a red light started to flash followed by a loud screeching sound.

He had just set off the alarm.

Chapter Thirty-Two

Sasha ran for the door, but Derek blocked her way once more. "How many times do I have to tell you to stop blocking me?! I'm going to save my family."

"That's not why I'm stopping you; you need to give everyone time to wake up. Give it a few seconds, if you run now you will be the only one out there. Wait until you hear some commotion."

"You mean the screams of people being attacked because you betrayed them."

"Sasha." He started, but she shook her head. She no longer wanted to hear anything he had to say.

It only took a few seconds before shouts and screams filled the air. "I'm going out now, and you cannot stop me."

"I won't; I'll try to clear you a path...Just get to the maze." He walked out before she could say anything else, not that she planned to. She waited a few seconds, giving him time to make a hole for her. She needed to make it to Cassie first, then Devin and Danny. They should be with Wendy, and together they would make it out of the house and away from this place.

The sounds of fighting slowly moved from the door, and she knew this was the only time she was going to get to escape. She created another shield and walked to the door.

She took a deep breath. She could do this; she needed to do this. With one last thought, she opened the door and peeked out. The dark hall was bathed in red lights every few seconds as the alarm continued to sound through the house. The once silent and clean hallway was filled with motionless bodies. Dent's filled the once smooth wall, chunks of wall scattered on the ground.

She looked down both sides of the hall, and there were no signs of Derek. She hoped he took them away from the stairs, that was the only way she knew she to get upstairs.

She silently crept down the hall, keeping her back flat against the wall. The darkness aided in hiding her from view. She finally made it to the stairs. She sunk low and started up them. She made it to the landing surprised she had yet to run into any of the attackers; though, it was a big house.

She crept down the hall until she reached her room. She slowly peeked in and bit back a gasp. Cassie was still there lying at the feet of an armed man with her eyes closed; there was a small line of blood flowing from her head. Around her neck was one of those wizard necklaces. Danny and Devin were both tied up Danny struggling to escape his binds and get to Cassie. Devin laid on his side with his back to her. She could see his arms bound behind his back as well.

She pulled her head back as the man turned to face the door. She needed to come up with a plan and fast.

She heard a radio go off to her left. Someone was coming up the stairs. She looked for a place to hide and ducked down next to a column. She hoped the darkness would keep her hidden enough to surprise him with an attack.

She wasn't strong enough to attack him by herself. She needed something to help her. He passed her, and she held her breath careful not to make a sound. There was a bust ten feet away. If she could grab it and hit him with it then maybe she had a chance.

She crept behind him and reached for the

bust. It was a lot heavier than she expected but she managed to pick it up and hurled it at his head. He went down with a loud thud a stream of blood flowed from the back of his head.

She swallowed the bile that rose in her throat at the thought of her actions.

She heard the door open behind her and whipped around and saw another guard. He raised his hand to attack, but Sasha reacted first. She felt power rush through her and aimed it directly at him. It hit him square in the chest and sent him flying into the room. He hit the wall with a thud, dropping to the ground and leaving a deep dent in his wake.

She ran into the room and shut the door behind her. She ran over to Danny and ripped off the necklace and untied him. She went to Cassie next while Danny tended to his twin.

"Where were you?!" Danny yelled untying Devin.

"I went downstairs to get tea before all of this started, and I ran into Derek. They set us up." She said pulling the necklace off Cassie and untying her.

"What do you mean they set this up?" Danny asked.

"I mean they planned this attack." She clarified.

"They're behind this?" Danny helped Devin to a sitting position.

"Yea." Sasha shook her head. "I feel so stupid."

"How did you get away?"

"He let me go. Created a diversion so I could come find you guys. Where's Wendy?" she looked around the room.

"I don't know. Once the alarm went off, I ran here but she was already out, and he took me down before I could do anything? They dragged Devin in a few second later." Danny explained.

"We need to get out of here." She turned back to Cassie and checked for a pulse. "It looks like they just knocked her out."

"We need a plan to get out of here," Danny said

"We need to go to the maze."

"Why there?" Devin asked finally coming to.

"Derek said that was where he was going to get us out."

Danny came over to Cassie and lifted her into his arms. "We can't trust him."

"I know that, but either way the maze

will make it easy for us to lose them."

"Sasha," Devin said. "We can't trust anything he told you."

"I know, but if you have a better plan, I'm all ears. This house is filled with who knows how many men, we need a way to get out and the front is not an option."

The twins shared a look before Danny relented. "Fine."

"Great." Sasha grabbed her journal from the night stand and headed towards the door. "Let's go!"

Chapter Thirty-Three

Sasha walked behind Devin and Danny, who had Cassie in his arms. They were heading down the back stairs. They had yet to run into an attacker, but they knew their luck would run out soon. They just needed to make it as close to the maze as they could before they were spotted.

Sasha bit back a gasp as they made it to

the landing, the bodies of Brandon's servants were lined up. Each wearing a wizard necklace, each dead, their face etched with fear.

They heard footsteps behind them, and they all ducked behind the long kitchen island. Sasha peaked around the corner and saw two men walking down the hall laugh as they dragged Wendy behind them. She was barely conscious; her hands and feet were bound. Her right eye was swollen shut, her lip was busted, and blood rolled down her face.

Sasha turned backed and saw Devin's fist glowing dark red. He was about to attack, but she reached out and grabbed his arm stopping him.

"Wait," she mouthed. He couldn't attack, they were greatly outnumbered, and they would never be able to win. He took a deep breath, calming his self-down.

They heard a door open and shut before the all let out a collective breath. "What do we do now?" she whispered.

The twins shrugged their shoulders. They wanted to save their mother, but they had an understanding. Wendy would always come back for her son, but her sons were never supposed to come back for her.

"We leave," Danny whispered adjusting Cassie in his arms.

"What about Wendy?" Sasha asked.

"They have her; Mom made us promise we would never come back for her. That we would always survive." Devin explained, his voice almost hollow.

Sasha nodded but did not say anything. She knew what they were feeling. She felt it herself when her mother gave herself up to save her. She was still feeling it, not knowing if she was dead or alive.

"Are you sure we can trust him and get to the maze?" Danny turned to her. "If we go out there and it's a trap, we could all die."

"We could die in here." Sasha reasoned.

They stood up, and Sasha helped Danny adjust Cassie in his arms. They walked towards the side door, hoping that it would lead them to the maze. They started to pick up their pace, but a loud explosion rocked the house sending the teens flying.

Sasha screamed as she landed on her wrist and Danny and Cassie were thrown clear across the room. But Danny had the forethought to create a shield just before they landed protecting them from most of the impact. Devin landed next to Sasha knocking his head on the wall. He rolled to his knees but swayed as he tried to stand.

"You ok?" Sasha reached out to him with her good hand.

"I think so..." he muttered as he kneeled, holding his head in his hands. His head exploded with pain. "Are you ok?"

"Yeah, I don't think it's broken." She motioned to her wrist.

"Good," he said shaking his head.

"Are you sure you're ok?"

"Yeah," he shook his head as he tried to stand, but fell back to his knees.

"Devin!" She reached out to him as another explosion rocked the house knocking both teens to the ground.

"We need to get out of here," Danny called over to them. He slowly stood to his feet lifting Cassie again and walked over to them as the house stopped shaking.

Devin groped the wall, trying to stand, and Sasha came to his side throwing his arm over her shoulder. They walked ahead of Danny, as they made their way to the side door. Devin pushed it open and peeked out. He couldn't see much – the darkness still blanketed the grounds.

"We need to stay close to each other and make it quick; the maze is about a hundred feet from the door." He whispered. They nodded and as quick as they could they ran for the maze.

Sasha kept her eyes on the entrance and with every step closer she felt hope fill her they were going to make it.

"Sir, I found them!" A voice rang through the dark night. The teens did not bother to look where it came from; they needed to keep running. If they stopped even for a second, they were done for. "They are headed towards the…" His voice faded as a jet of red flames, that seemed to come out of nowhere, hit him square in the chest with enough force to send him flying back another twenty feet or so. His screams filled the air as the flames consumed his chest.

She turned and looked over her shoulder to see where the flame came from. Running towards them she could make out…Derek! She couldn't help the small jolt of happiness that filled her seeing him alive.

They finally made it into the maze, but they didn't stop running. They needed to get to the other end as quickly as possible. They weaved through the narrow passage ways

until they came to the direct center and
Sasha stopped.

"Why are you stopping?" Danny asked.

"He told me to go where he trained me.
This is it."

"Where do we go from here?"

"I...I don't know?" Sasha stuttered.

"He didn't tell you where to go after
this?" Danny yelled.

"No... just said go where he trained me."
She looked for the right words.

"Sasha!" Derek's voice broke through as
he ran into the center of the maze. His
clothes were torn, and he was bleeding from
side – it looked like he had a black eye
forming on his right eye. Before she knew
what was happening, he pulled her into his
arms, and he was kissing her. For a split
second, she forgot where she was and what
they were going through. All she felt was his
lips on her, his hands on her waist holding
her to him before it was ended just as
quickly.

"Get off her!" Devin yanked Derek off
her and tossed him back a few feet.

"Devin!" Sasha screamed.

"No, we want answers!" Danny yelled
placing Cassie down next to Sasha. The

twins stood in front of the girls. "What the hell did you do?"

Derek shook his head. "We don't have much time we need to get out of here. I will explain everything later, but we need to go now!"

"Why should we trust you? You're the reason we are running for our lives again!" Devin shot back.

"I know, and I'm sorry! But it was going to happen regardless, so I made an escape plan." Derek tried to explain.

"You could have told us! That was an option!" Danny yelled.

"Look! I thought I had a few more days; my father told me they were not going to attack until you were on the move. I was going to warn you guys the night before. Make sure you leave before anything could happen and that you took Cassie with you. I have a jeep behind the maze; I was slowly filling it with food and supplies for you guys. I did not know anything changed until tonight." Sasha knew he was lying, he never planned to save all of them, just her but right now was not the best time to point that out.

There was another explosion that shook

the ground. The teens looked up, Brandon Barons home crumbled to the ground.

"Mom!" Danny yelled and made for the house, but Derek stopped him.

"She's alive," Derek said. "I saw them drag her out to a truck.

Danny screamed in frustration and turned to Derek! "This is all your fault! You helped your father betray us!"

"I'm sorry I really am. I thought I had time to get you all away." Derek lied. "But if you want to get away, we need to leave now!" he urged.

"Guys they could find us any second. We do need to leave." Sasha agreed.

The twins looked at one another having a silent conversation. "Fine," Devin agreed for them. "But," he reached into his pocket and grabbed the wizard necklace he was forced to wear. "You have to wear this at all times."

"Fine." Derek allowed Devin to put on the necklace. "This way." He walked around them and down another narrow passage. Danny picked up Cassie, and they followed Derek. Sasha noted that he was quick even with his injuries. They came to a side wall, and he stopped.

There was male voice getting closer to them.

"Through this ledge. On the other side is a slope that goes down about twenty feet. Be prepared to slide so don't scream." He explained.

"I'll go first." Devin pushed through the hedge. He let out a small yelp, and he rolled down the hill.

"Sasha you're next," Danny said. Sasha pushed through the hedges and bit back the scream as she slid down the slope; her wrist screamed in pain when she landed at the base. Devin helped her to her feet as she got her bearings. A few second later Derek slid down; then Cassie, then Danny.

The jeep was similar to the one Sasha and Cassie used to get to Wendy's home. This one was a few years newer and a bit bigger.

They loaded in the truck, Danny placed Cassie behind the driver seat and climbed in behind the wheel. Devin sat next to him in the passenger seat. Sasha took a seat next to her and Derek was on her other side.

"Where are we supposed to go?" Sasha asked. "Everyone we know has been taken in, and we can't go back to your home. They most likely know about that."

"Let's just get away from here, and we can worry about that later." Danny started the jeep and drove off through the woods.

Sasha felt Derek slide his hand on to hers and interlocked their fingers. She felt him squeeze her hand, but she couldn't bring herself to look at him. Instead, she leaned her head on Cassie's shoulder and looked out the window.

Chapter Thirty-Four

They drove all night and into the next morning.

Sasha flipped through her mother's journal, happy that she remembered to bring it with her. It was the last piece of her mother she had left.

After the first day of driving they shut the radio off. Every station was playing the same story of the traitor Brandon Baron. The country was shocked to find out the Royal Historian was a part of the group looking to over throw them. The report stated that Brandon was killed in the fight. Jasmine's twin sister Wendy was taken alive along with a few of the other employees of Baron's. What shocked the world more was the extent of the group. Cassie's parents were arrested along with a few others who were a part of the true royal guards. The whereabouts of Sasha and Cassie along with Wendy's twin sons Danny and Devin were unknown at the time. But they were creating road blocks along all major roads to find them.

Half way into the day Cassie finally woke up, much to Sasha's and Danny's delight. It took a bit for her to calm down after they explained what happened.

The safe house that Danny and Devin said they could go to was too far to drive to. With the number of people looking for them, it was too risky to drive on unfamiliar roads. They needed to wait until the heat died down a bit before they could make the journey. The group of teens worked to figure out where they could go and lay low for a few days until it was safe for them to travel on the open road again.

After a few hours of endless debate, and every idea of Derek's being shot down, Danny finally pulled under some trees, and they decided to get some sleep. They decided they would try to think of a new plan when they were not running on fumes. Sasha slept for a bit, but her mind would not let her sleep for long.

She felt like she was missing something but she could not for the life of her figure out what it was. She hoped flipping through the journal would cause her to see something that would jog her memory. But she had no luck thus far.

She read the entry of her mother's last couple of days at the castle. She liked the story; it showed who her mother truly was. Her mother had saved a maid, her good friend Amie, from being attacked.

She skimmed the story until she got to the bottom, she was about to turn the page, but Derek grabbed her hand.

"Wait!" He whispered.

"Are you reading over my shoulder?" She looked up at him.

"I'm trying to but it's not working, your book doesn't make sense. But did you notice that?" He pointed to the bottom of the page.

"Notice what?"

"Those numbers at the bottom of the page." He pointed the erased number at the bottom.

"Yeah, but they're gone."

"Those numbers were pressed into the page." He pointed out. "She wrote them hard enough that they would still be legible. They might be important. What is the entry about?"

"My mom saved one of her friends from an awful fate when she was working at the castle," Sasha replied nonchalantly.

"What type of fate?" Derek asked.

"A group of Guards cornered her, and my mom saved her from them."

"The numbers are long enough to be coordinates. If that entry is about her saving her friend from a terrible fate that friend might be willing to help her daughter out of a dangerous situation of her own." He pointed out.

"Even after all these years?"

"You said your mother said everything in this journal was here to help you."

"Yeah, but she erased the numbers..."

"After she printed them so hard on the page they would be there later. Is there anything else in the book like that?"

"No."

"Then it's in there for a reason." Derek surmised. "We need a map."

"Where are we going to get a map?"

"I packed one in the glove compartment." He said.

"Devin," Sasha leaned forward and softly shook him. "Wake up!"

"Sasha, what?" Devin groaned opening his eyes.

"I need the map from the glove

compartment," Sasha whispered.

"What? Why?" He blinked rubbing the sleep from his eyes.

"I think I found a somewhere for us to go."

Devin blinked a few more times and opened the glove compartment. He grabbed the map and handed it to Sasha.

She opened the map and focused on the numbers.

"There!" Derek pointed to a spot after a minute of looking.

"That's in Eolia. How far of the drive do you think it is for here?"

"At least another day maybe two since we need to stay off the main roads."

"Guys wake up!" Sasha shook Cassie as Devin woke his twin. "I think I found a safe place for us to go. It was in my Mom's journal."

"Where?" Danny asked stretching his arms above his head.

"I found coordinates in my journal. Well, Derek pointed them out to me, but either way, I think I found somewhere else for us to go." She pointed to the map.

"It's in Eolia," Devin said.

"Yeah, she has a friend, Amie Chiabse

who she saved from being attacked. At the bottom of the page where these coordinates pressed on the page."

"How do we know he didn't do it?" Danny glared at Derek.

"Because I saw these the first time I read the journal at your house before they came. I just never realized what they were." Sasha said.

"And she is someone your mother trusted?" Devin asked.

"Yeah, I guess it's been years, but she left it in the journal. She must think Amie is someone we can trust today."

"Let's go," Danny wiped his eyes and sat up in his chair.

"Just like that?"

"If you swear those numbers were there before we met him then I trust it," Danny said.

"Yeah, they've been there."

"I trust your Mom. If she said this is a safe place, then this is a safe place. Or at least our best shot."

Chapter Thirty-Five

They drove straight for a day and a half taking every back road on the map and switching between Danny and Devin. They refused to let Derek drive, and he was fine with that, he was content to sit next to Sasha. They made it to the outskirts of Eolia when Devin finally pulled over.

"We need a phone directory to find her address."

"We could take one out of a phonebook," Danny suggested.

"All of us don't need to go," Devin stated. "I'll go, and if I am not back within an hour then run."

"You'll be back," Danny growled at his twin.

"I'll go with you," Derek suggested.

"No," Devin answered. "They may know my name but not my face. No one will ID me."

"He has a point," Sasha said.

Derek nodded and leaned back in his

seat. Devin hopped out of the jeep and walked off toward town. He was gone for an agonizing thirty minutes before he returned.

"There is only 1 Amie Chiabse living in this town. I found the address." He held up the sheet.

"Then let's go." Sasha was impatient to get indoors.

Devin got behind the wheel and checked the address and against the map. "Looks like we are a short drive away."

"Good! I'm ready to get out of this car." Cassie sighed.

"I second that!" Sasha agreed.

Devin started the jeep and started through the town. It was pretty late in the night, not many people out which worked for them. They drove for another ten minutes before Devin pulled over. "That's the house." Devin pointed to a two-level home. Sasha could make out a garden out front and a few potted plants sitting on the steps. There was a bay window to the right of the stairs that had the curtains drawn. There were no lights on in the house, at least not where they could see.

"I'll go up," Sasha said.

"I'll go with you," Derek suggested, but

Sasha shook her head.

"No, it will be better if I go by myself. She's more likely to open the door if it's a lone female standing there versus a group."

"She right." Devin agreed.

Derek's shoulders sagged slightly. "Ok, um but run at the first sign of trouble."

Sasha nodded and got out of the jeep. She jogged over to the house, rang the bell and gave a soft knocked on the door. Loud enough for the occupant to hear but no one else.

She bounced on the balls of her feet as she waited to hear movement behind the door. After a long few seconds, she rang the bell a few more times when a feeling a dread filled her body. *What if she wasn't alone? What if she was married and had children of her own.* They never discuss the chances that she could be married or had a family. If she did, then there was a greater chance that she would not be willing to help them. Not that she would help them in the first place.

She heard a few sounds come from the other side of the door before she heard a soft, timid voice. "Who's there?"

"Hi… Umm, can you open the door?"

"No! It's the middle of the night, and

you are ringing my door bell and banging on my door. Now tell me who you are before I call the Enforcers!" The reply was sharp.

Sasha paused and thought, she had no idea what Amie looked like. This could be the wrong person, and she could out herself and get them all killed.

"Before I tell you who I am, can you tell me if you are Amie Chiabse? That's who I'm looking for."

There was a huff before she answered. "Yes I am Amie, now you have two seconds to tell me who you are before I call the Enforcers. I'm already half way there on the phone!"

"Please don't call the Enforcers! Y-you knew my mother." Sasha rushed out

"I've known a lot of people."

There was no way she could get Amie to open the door without telling her everything. She just hoped that she wasn't making a mistake that could cost her, her life.

"You knew my Mom from the castle, umm she wrote about you in her journal. She saved you from being …raped." She finished.

There was no sound for a moment. Sasha started to take a step back when the sound of locks clicking. 'A lot of locks' she noted before the front door swung open.

Amie was not what she pictured at all, she was tall at least 6'1-6'2, and she was built. Not like a man, but she was fit. Sasha noted the outline of muscles through the fabric of Aime's night shirt. Her hair was cut short, and her face was covered in old scars.

"Sasha!" Amie looked down at her a look of shock and bewilderment on her face.

Sasha nodded looking up Amie.

"You are here?" Amie added.

"And I'm hoping that you are a friend and that I can come in and hide." Sasha looked over her shoulder.

"Are you being followed?" Amie looked over Sasha's shoulder into the woods.

"Yes…" but she shook her head, "I mean no."

Amie held up the bat in her hands. "Is it yes or no?"

"It's both," Sasha said. "It's my friends; they are waiting for a signal if you are friend or foe."

"Your mother saved my life; I can save yours, tell them to come." She put the bat down.

"Thank you!" Sasha jumped and latched on to Amie giving her hug. She turned to the jeep and motioned for them to come.

"Tell them to pull the jeep into the garage," Amie said as she pointed to the side of the house.

Sasha ran down the stairs, back over to the jeep.

"Pull into the garage," Sasha told Devin and headed back up to the house. Amie opened the garage door, and Devin pulled the jeep in. Amie shut it behind them.

After a few minutes, they were all standing in Amie's living room.

"Thank you." Sasha beamed.

"I've owed Jasmine so much more, how long do you need to stay?"

"Just a few days until we can rest up and make a new plan to go back into hiding," Danny explained.

"I'm happy to help in any way I can," Amie said. "Your mother," she turned to Sasha. "Is an amazing woman. I know everything they are reporting about her is a lie. But it's late, and you all look exhausted." She stood. "How about a hot shower and good night's rest. In the morning, we will sit down and fully talk about this. I will put towels in the bathroom; it's down the hall." She looked the teens up and down. "Do you have a change of clothes?"

"No," Derek answered. "I was not able to get them before the attack."

"You mean before your family betrayed us." Devin snipped.

"Stop." Sasha gave them a stern look. "As much as you don't like it, he is the only reason we escaped; it was his father's choice to do what he did. Derek saved us and arguing with him over what we can't change is not going to help us."

Devin stayed quiet, but Danny just shook his head.

"Ok," Amie brought their attention back to her. "I think I might have some clothes that can fit you in my basement. Sasha and Cassie can use the shower in my room. I will have some clothes set out for you both." She turned and reached into the closet next to the bathroom and grabbed a hand full of towels. She handed one to Sasha and Cassie and pointed them towards her bedroom before turning to the boys and handing them towels as well.

"Sasha and Cassie will share the

bedroom down the hall. You three can share the living room; I will bring out bedding while you guys shower." She explained. The boys nodded, and Amie headed towards the basement.

Thirty minutes later Sasha and Cassie were showered, changed, and in bed. Sasha would never know if Cassie asked her anything that night. The moment her head touched the pillow, she was out like a light.

Chapter Thirty-Six

Sasha woke up to the sound of Cassie's light snores. She looked over at the clock, 8 am. She slept for nine hours straight for the first time in days, and she felt so refreshed.

She slowly slid out of bed, stretching as she stood. She hoped Amie was awake or at least would not mind her getting something to eat. She was starving.

She walked out the room and headed for the kitchen. It had a small television in there, and if she kept the volume low, maybe she would not wake anyone.

She crept past Amie's door and the boys sleeping in the living room. Danny was sleeping on the smaller couch closest to their room. Devin was sleeping on the couch against the wall, and Derek was on the floor between them. She walked down the small hallway and into the kitchen.

She turned on the small TV set; careful to make sure the volume was low.

There wasn't much on this early in the

morning; she flipped through the channels landing on the news. They were talking about the castle getting ready for the Vector dinner taking place in a few days. As well as a huge announcement the Royals were going to make. They wanted the entire kingdom to hear about it at the live dinner they were hosting afterward.

Sasha rolled her eyes; whatever the announcement was, there was no way it was going in her favor. She flipped the channels – no need to waste any more brain cells than she needed on them. She settled on an old children's cartoon and walked to the fridge.

With her stomach rumbling, she decided to cook breakfast for everyone. She hoped Amie would be ok with that. *What should I make* she perused the contents of the fridge? She had eggs and bacon, green onions and some shredded cheese.

"I didn't take you for a cartoon type of girl."

Sasha jumped and turned to the kitchen doorway. Derek stood in the entry way, his arms folded over his chest, sleep still written over his face.

"What are you doing up?"

He shrugged. "I heard the TV; I wanted

to see who was up?"

"Oh, well it's just me," she gave a nervous laugh. "You can go back to sleep."

"I was waking up anyway." He took a seat at the table. "The floor is not that comfortable." He shrugged.

"Oh, yeah. I guess it's not. I'm sorry about that." She placed the breakfast ingredients on the counter.

"Eh." He waved it off. "I get it. It's their way of punishing me, so I'll deal with it."

"Really?" she raised an eyebrow.

"Yeah, it's not much they can do to me seeing as though we are all in the same boat. Taking the couch and leaving me the floor is all they can do to me right now, so I will take it. I mean this is my fault." He paused, but she did not correct him, much to his displeasure. "I know, I should have come forward earlier, I know I should have told you what he was planning."

"You knew and did nothing to stop it. One hint, one word, and this could all be different."

"Or it could all be the same, or worse. Sasha." He came closer, and she took a step back, her lower back hitting the counter top. His arms came to rest on either side of her caging her in. "I never wanted to hurt you. I was in over my head…I thought I could fix it, I thought-"

"You thought wrong." She looked up at him, trying to keep the nervousness he caused at bay.

He dropped his head, his forehead almost touching hers. "I know." He sighed. She saw his eyes flicker to her lips then her eyes. He bit his lip and slid his hands over hers and slowly up her arms; he ran them over her neck until he cupped her face. Sasha brought her hand up to his, holding on to his wrists. He leaned in slightly, and she knew, he was going to kiss her, in the middle of their messed up situation and conversation. In the middle of what they were going through, he was going to kiss her again.

Even after everything he did, with everything going on, at that moment none of those things matter and Sasha realized she wanted him to kiss her. "The first time you kissed me, it was after you betrayed us." She whispered halting his movements. He shut his eyes squeezing them tightly and dropped his forehead on hers.

"I know." He whispered.

"Why did you kiss me then?"

"Because I didn't know." He kissed her forehead. "I didn't know if I would make it or…or if you would. It might have been my last chance."

"And now?" she asked leaning into him. He ran his thumb over her bottom lip. "Because I don't want to waste any more time not being with you." He leaned down and pressed his lips firmly against hers. Her eyes closed and she pushed out all negative thoughts out of her head and pressed her lips more firmly against his.

Derek stepped closer, and she let her hands fall to his chest gripping his shirt between her fingers. One hand fell to her waist and gave it tight squeeze forcing her tighter against him. His other hand drifted into her hair tilting her head back allowing him to deepen the kiss.

Sasha slid her hands up around his neck pulling him closer. His hands ran down her waist gripping her thighs. He effortlessly lifted her up, setting her on the counter, and stepped between her legs. She pulled him in, and his mouth drifted from her lips to her jaw making his way to her neck. Her head fell back giving him more access while his hands slid under her shirt.

"Ahem," Amie coughed from the doorway breaking their moment. Derek took a step back from the counter, and Sasha hopped down.

"Good morning." Sasha smoothed down her hair. Looking anywhere but at Amie, hoping to avoid the awkward conversation she knew was coming her way. "I was just making everyone breakfast."

"Let me guess he was helping?" Amie rolled her eyes. "Teenagers," she yawned. "But is now really the best time for that?" She waved her hand between them.

"...No, it's not," Sasha dropped her head avoiding Derek's gaze.

"I'm going to shower," Derek said stiffly, walking out of the room not sparing Sasha a glance. She watched him go until he passed Amie's shoulder.

"So..." Amie took a seat at the table.

"So?" Sasha turned to the counter.

"You two are together?"

"...No... not really," she shook her head.

"It looked like you are."

"It's too complicated to explain," Sasha said as she started cracking the eggs.

"Do you like him?"

"Yes...I do but like I said it's

complicated."

"Well from what I just saw it doesn't look too complicated."

Sasha dropped her hands to her side and turned around. "It's just …um…I don't know if I can trust him. I know how I feel about him, but at the same time, I don't. I sound like a broken record saying this, but his family is the reason we are on your doorstep. They betrayed us, and he knew about it. Yes, he saved us, but he broke my trust, and the trust of everyone I care about so I don't know what to do."

"Well, I see how he feels about you."

"Yeah," she sniffed. "I know, but this is all so confusing right now. I'm not in a place to make decisions about anything. I mean I'm sixteen, and everything around me is going to hell, and a boy is the last distraction I need."

Amie pondered for a few moments. "I would agree but, it looks like you're not following your own line of thinking at least not from what I could see."

"I have a handle on it…I think." She whispered the last part.

"You are still a teenager. You are allowed to make reckless decisions.

Just remember the effects your decisions will have on everyone. But that is not the reason I came in here." She stood and clasped her hands. "After you, all went to sleep last night; I fished this out." She walked over to the corner and picked up a small wooden box; well-worn and covered in dust. "This belonged to your mother."

Chapter Thirty-Seven

"My Mom?" She looked down at the box.

Amie nodded, "She gave it to me after I was set up here. She must have been a few months pregnant with you. I could never open it, she sealed it and told me only a family member could open it. She wanted to protect me from the contents."

"So you think I can open it?" Sasha stared at the latch.

"That's my guess."

Sasha placed the box on the counter, breakfast long forgotten. "Should pull the top up?"

Amie shrugged.

Sasha grasped the edges of the box lifted but no luck. The top would not budge. "Well, that didn't work." She took a step back after a few seconds. "How else do you propose I open it?"

Amie shrugged. "You got me. You're her daughter. You should be able to open it."

"Why couldn't she make this easy?" Sasha muttered. She ran her hand over the top and around the edge. "Ow!" she hissed, jerking her hand away and inspecting her finger.

"What happened?" Amie asked.

"Splinter." Sasha brought the finger to her mouth and sucked trying to pull out the splinter of wood with her teeth. "It's bleeding."

"Try that." Amie urged.

"My blood?" Sasha questioned.

"You are her daughter. I normally wouldn't suggest this but since you are already bleeding...."

Sasha hesitated a bit before she held her finger over the box and gave it a squeeze. One small bright red drop fell from her finger onto the box.

They watched in amazement as the blood landed with a small plop and was absorbed into the box. After a few seconds, the latch popped and the lid slowly started to rise.

"It worked!" Sasha exclaimed, both gleeful and astonished.

"What worked?" Devin asked walking into the room rubbing the sleep from his eyes.

"Good morning to you too," Sasha greeted as she opened the lid completely. "Amie gave me this box from my Mom. Apparently, my blood opens it."

"A blood locks…not common, but it has its uses." He noted.

"Of course you know about this," Sasha said dryly pulling out the envelope on top and opening it.

"What else is in there?" Devin reached around her and pulled out some folded paper flipping through them. "What does that say?" He nodded to the letter in her hands.

Sasha ran her fingers over the hand written letter, taking in her mother's handwriting before finally reading it aloud.

'I am sorry; this is not a letter I ever planned to write nor is it a letter I ever want you to read. My child, at this moment I do not know if you are to be a girl or a boy or if you will ever live to read this letter. Part of me wishes you will never read what is in the box. In here is the truth, the complete truth, about everything. This life I am running from, this life I dread, is not a life I want to bring you into. Children are so innocent they have no choice of the life that is theirs. You never asked for this; you never

*wanted to be born. I made the mistake of
creating you knowing the price you must
pay. I should have never done this you.*

*The first thing I must tell you is the
hardest. I do not know when you will read
this or if you ever will but on the off chance
you do, you deserve the truth. Sam, the man
who will raise you with me. My husband
who will always be the love of my life is not
your father, at least not in the biological
sense. Prince Alessandro is your biological
father, and I must tell you it was done on
purpose."*

"What?" Sasha exhaled as the letter fell
to the table. She felt sick. Her mother had to
be lying to her. Right? Otherwise, this did
not make sense.

Devin reached for the letter, but Sasha
picked it up first. "No."

"You need to finish it." Devin pushed.

"Did you not just hear what I read?" she
looked up at him. "He's my father. And she
did it on purpose. I don't want to know what
else she has to say. How could she do this?"

"You will never know if you don't
finish," Amie said softly. "I knew your
mother around that time; she was a very
smart woman. There was no way she would

not have a reason behind her actions."

Sasha shook her head; she could not fathom her mother being this person. She could not see her mother as someone who would decide to have a child as a pawn. A child with someone who was trying to kill her. Sasha steeled herself as she continued.

This is not easy for me to write to you. It's my fault; my family is gone. I put them in danger, and I will never forgive myself for that. I let my anger consume me. The anger of what happened to my great grandmother. The fact we lost the crown, that we must endure living in fear. So, I devised a plan, a plan to get close to Alessandro and get pregnant with his child. It was not easy nor am I proud of my actions, but I am grateful for you as you grow inside my body.

My plan was to do to them what they did to us. To have a child and have them claim it but I was young and stupid. I did not think it all the way through. I did not account for the fact that I was putting a greater price on your head at the time. It wasn't until I was pregnant with you that I realized what I had done, that I made you a pawn in this game... in their game. I realized you would grow up knowing the reason I had you was to use you as a pawn against what would now be your family.

I knew I needed to get as far away as I could to protect you. My hope is I can provide you with a normal life. With the life, you deserve to have, a life away from all the pain and fear that comes with our bloodline.

I promise you when you grow up, and you reach the correct age I will tell you the truth. I will tell you all that I have written in this letter. I truly hope you never have to learn any of this before your father and I have a chance to explain why we did what we did.

I must not be too optimistic otherwise I have no reason to write this letter. On the great chance, I am not with you to explain or give you the option to make some decisions on your own I leave you this box. This is my last resort box. In here is all the information I know regarding the castle from working there. The pathways I used that can only be accessed by a true member of the royal family. No one knows about these. I do not know if any of this information will come in handy to you. I hope you will never have to use what is in this box.

*Please know that I love you. Where ever
I am in the world I want you to know I love
you with all that I am. You are my child, and
I hope I did everything in my power to
protect you. If I am no longer on this Earth,
I pray that you are safe with Amie and you
will never give up."*

"You're Alessandro's daughter," Devin
whispered. "You're Alessandro's
daughter." He repeated excitedly as if it
explained everything.

Amie's eyes widened understanding
Devin's line of thought. "You are
Alessandro's daughter."

"Can one of you guys tell me what you
are thinking because I am lost?" She looked
between the two of them. "Last time I check
that was a bad thing. It's another reason for
them to want me dead."

"Yes, but you do not see the other side,"
Devin explained. "The Annual Vector's
meeting is coming up. Right?" He looked to
Amie for confirmation, and she nodded.
"The dinner part is televised; they have
other celebrities and well to do people there
as well."

"I know, I've watched it before," Sasha

answered still missing the point.

Derek shook his head. "You are not getting it, Sasha. You are a Princess, the *only* princess. The ballroom will be filled with the most important and influential people in the entire kingdom. If you go into the room and announce in front of all of them, and on live television, that you are Alessandro's daughter the whole kingdom will hear at once. There is no way they can get rid of you in front of all those people. You can claim they are trying to kill you and everyone who knew the truth. There is proof your mother worked in the castle around that time, they have already stated to that fact. You can say all they need to do is a blood test in a public area and you can prove you're Alessandro's daughter. It might not get you the crown, but it will get them off our back."

"Exactly!" Amie nodded.

Sasha shook her head in disbelief. "No."

"No, what?" Danny asked walking into the room scratching his head, sleep still prevalent in his eyes.

"No to going to the castle," Sasha answered firmly.

"Why would we go to the castle, I

thought we agreed on finding a new place to live?" he questioned, taking a seat the kitchen table.

"Yea but we might have a new plan." Devin looked at Sasha.

"With Jasmine's help."

"I'm confused, or maybe I'm just that tired," Danny said as he rubbed his eyes. "But how did Jasmine help with this plan?"

"She didn't, well not really," Sasha spoke up. "She left me this box, and there was a letter for me, well not really me just her unborn child..."

"Which turned out to be you, so it was written to you." Devin interrupted her train of thought.

"Anyway," Sasha rolled her eyes. "It turns out I'm Alessandro's daughter, and she got pregnant with me on purpose-"

"Holy shit!" Danny snorted. "Tell me you're joking. Why would she do that?"

"Well, she said her plan was to do to them what they did to our family, but once she realized what she did, she decided that bringing a child into this world for her own selfish purpose was not fair ...well to me."

"So what is the plan?" Danny cracked

his neck and rolled his shoulders trying to wake up.

"Jasmine left us maps from her time working in the castle with all the secret passage ways. Now I haven't checked them out yet, but if she used them, we have a good shot at getting in."

"And what, there are still only five of us, we wouldn't stand a chance in attacking the castle."

Sasha took over. "The plan wouldn't be to fight. It would be to crash the Vector's dinner and tell the world the truth. Tell them I am Alessandro's daughter and that is why they are trying to kill me."

"It's perfect." Devin looked at his twin. "They already stated Jasmine was working there at that time. Basically, everyone they have arrested knows the truth about who Jasmine really is. We could spin it saying they were covering their tracks. They are trying to get rid of everyone who knows the truth."

"What about, Jasmine killing three guards?" Danny asked.

"I could come forward. Those men were notorious for unwanted touching and messing with the maids. I know there are complaints about them and other maids who were attacked. Jasmine acted in self-defense for me." Amie suggested.

"Let me make sure I get this right. You want to break into the castle when it has the most influential people in the entire kingdom altogether. Then somehow get to the ballroom and in front of the entire world tell them Sasha is Alessandro's daughter?" Danny asked.

"We have to figure out all the details of how, but yes, that's the plan," Devin confirmed.

"They won't attack her, not while she's unarmed, not in front of the cameras and the guest there," Amie answered. "I worked there for years; I still have friends who work there. They are all about appearances."

"Even though they want me dead. What would stop them from arresting me right there?" Sasha asked.

"They will try and arrest you but when you first sneak in you will be able to say what you need to before anyone realizes what is going on."

"Could this work?" Sasha looked at the faces around her. *There must be a catch.*

"I think this would be the only chance

we would have to save our family from a life in prison or death," Devin said quietly. "And this will only work with you."

Sasha looked at him. "You know if this doesn't work we all will die."

"It's a risk. A huge risk but I had a few days of freedom. A few days of a somewhat normal life where every extra sound didn't cause us to be scared. Where we were not living in a cave. The only time we ever went to town was for supply runs, and even then, we were full of fear. Fear of who might see us. Always told to keep to ourselves. Now, there is a chance at life where we are not always looking over our shoulder waiting for the other shoe to drop. Sasha, you had that life, a normal life with friends and parties and a real school. I want that life Sasha, my brother and I deserve that life. We have done nothing wrong. This is not fair!" Devin's hands shook at the end of his rant. Danny reached over and grasped his brother's shoulder giving it a squeeze. "I don't want to live in fear anymore Sasha." He whispered. "We have a way out."

Sasha thought it over in and sighed. "I guess we need a plan."

Chapter Thirty-Eight

"So we go to sleep with no plan and wake up with this plan?" Cassie took a sip of her orange juice.

"Seems like it," Derek said.

"I know it's a long shot but what choice to do we have? If we don't do this, our parents could die, and we will live on the run for the rest of our lives."

"And if we do this, there is a chance that we die," Cassie said.

"Small chance," Devin said. "But I don't think we will."

"Just go over everything," Cassie said.

Devin laid out all the material on the living room floor. "We only have a few days to pull this off."

"If we can pull this off," Danny muttered, but they ignored him, Cassie shifted next to him.

"I've looked at the maps. From what I read, and what Amie remembers, they are still accurate."

"So where do we enter?" Sasha asked.

"There." He pointed to a dot on the map. "This is off the cliff, and there's the door to the secret walkway that will take us to Gabriela's old room."

"Which they are using as storage space, normally they do not patrol this room," Amie interjected.

"Even after all these years later," Derek asked, and Amie nodded.

"So we enter there, and a bit down the hall there is a small entrance to a few other passage ways."

"Aren't those halls guarded?"

"Not much," Amie answered again. "After what happened with Gabriela, they closed off that wing of the castle. They don't use it much. From what I remember, the guards make their rounds every hour but other than that; they mostly stay away."

"Which is perfect. The entrance to the tunnel is only 30 feet away at most. We get in and follow it around until we get to the door in the banquet hall. From there you make your announcement and then...."

"Then we die." Danny finished.

"Danny!" Sasha scolded.

"What! We were all thinking it." He

defended. "They could just attack us and say it was self-defense. The world already thinks we are out to kill them. We need to understand that this is a possible outcome."

"Anyway." Devin got back on track. "We guard Sasha when she enters. I guess once we show up there will be a bit of confusion, and that should be enough time for her to make the announcement."

"Then we die," Danny added

"Danny!" Cassie swatted him on the arm. "Not helping."

"Sorry." He rubbed the sore spot. "I do have a question though. If we need to enter off the side of a cliff, which looks from the map is facing the ocean, how do we get there?"

"By boat," Devin answered.

"And where are we getting a boat from?" Danny countered.

"I will rent it," Amie answered. "It should be fairly easy to do so."

"So we have the plan..." Sasha said. "When do we leave?"

"Well the meeting is in two days, so I say in twenty minutes," Devin answered.

"That soon?" Cassie asked.

Devin nodded. "This will be the only

shot where we can get in front of enough people and tell our truth. The networks will broadcast this all over the nation, and it will be too big for them to cover up."

"Do you think anyone will believe me?" Sasha asked.

"I'm not sure." Devin shrugged. "But we need them to."

Chapter Thirty-Nine

They were almost to the castle. She could see it from her vantage point. In another ten minutes, they would be ready to disembark and start what could be the end of their lives. She shook her head; she couldn't think like that, she needed to stay positive. She knew the truth. She just needed to get everyone else to believe it as well.

She looked around the boat. Amie was steering, Devin was next to her with the map. Danny and Cassie were huddled together, and Derek was sitting across from her. She could feel his eyes on her - they had been on her most of the night.

She shook her head trying to clear her thoughts and calm her nerves. It helped to remember why she was here. This was their last chance to make everything right. Even though they had a plan, the odds were stacked against them. She rubbed her hands on her dark jeans trying to shake off the last bit of nervousness when she felt Derek sit down next to her.

"Sasha." He whispered, but she kept her head down. "Look at me." His voice soft and warm in the cold night air.

She lifted her gaze. "Yes?"

He opened his mouth to speak, but Devin spoke first to the group. "We're here." He whispered to the group. Sasha kept her eyes on Derek; he shook his head keeping his thoughts to himself.

Amie anchored the boat behind some large rocks. Hopefully, they were large enough to keep the boat from being seen. The gap from the boat to the rocks wasn't too large. Quickly and quietly, they jumped from the boat to the rocks; each one landing with a soft thump.

"Here's the path." Devin pointed out. "Right where she said it would be."

"I guess that means everything will probably be the same," Danny said.

"I hope so." Cassie shivered. "So can we get a move on, it's freezing out here."

They started up the path to the castle, their steps illuminated by the moon light. By now everyone should be seated and the dinner was about to begin.

They walked the path in silence, only the

sound of the ocean knocking against the rocks could be heard.

After twenty minutes of hiking, they finally reached the wall. Devin placed his hand on the stone, and his hand glowed a bright pink. The rock shook slightly before it slowly slid out of the way.

Thankfully the waves knocking against the seabed drowned out the sound. Sasha walked through the narrow opening first with the rest following behind her. Devin brought up the rear closing the opening behind them. Derek made a few balls of lights in his hand and spread them out in front of them. They continued in silence through the hidden tunnel.

They headed up the slight slope of another tunnel for about fifteen minutes until they reached the wall that would lead them into the castle.

Sasha put her hand on the wall and hesitated, "There's no turning back once we go through this door."

"Open it," Danny said grasping Cassie's hand tightly.

She felt Derek squeeze her free hand for reassurance, her hand glowed a pale pink, and the wall shook for a few seconds before the bricks starting rearranging creating an opening.

Slowly the bricks started moved to form an opening. They walked in the room where it all started as the opening closed behind them.

"The next passage is down the hall about twenty feet from this door." Devin pointed out on the map.

"Let's get this over with," Danny said shuffling his feet from side to side.

Amie walked to the door and opened it a crack. "Looks like the coast is clear." She said ushering them to the door. They slipped passed her and into the hall. Quickly and quietly, they rushed down the hall to the next hidden door.

"It should be around here somewhere," Devin whispered running his hand over the wall. "It should feel slightly raised."

They all lined up to the wall running their hands over it.

"This is taking longer than expected," Derek muttered after a few minutes.

"I know," Devin muttered. "But it has to be here." He said as he moved further down the wall.

"This is taking too long…the next shift

could come any second." Sasha said in a hushed tone then froze as the sound of footsteps echoed through the hall.

"Someone's coming." Derek hissed. "We need to find this door."

"I'm trying, but I am not finding it," Devin whispered.

"You said it was around here; the footsteps are getting closer." Derek hissed back.

"The book said it should be here, and we are going as fast as we can," Devin argued back, and the rest of the group tensed as the footsteps sounded from the corner.

"They're getting closer," Sasha whispered speeding up her search.

"Here!" Devin breathed out as his hand glowed a bright pink and the door quickly opened. They all rushed through, and Devin closed the door behind them right as the guard turned the corner.

"That was too close." Cassie huffed leaning on Danny a bit.

"Yea it was." Sasha pushed off the wall. "But we need to hurry up." She glanced at Derek's watch. "It's already taken us twice as long to get here. We need to make sure we get there in time."

"Yeah, if we don't hurry we might miss all of the reception," Devin said taking the lead down the tunnel with everyone following behind him.

They jogged down the path until they came to the opening.

"This way." Devin headed down the path to the right. They ran for only a short time before Devin stopped in front of a small doorway. "This is it."

"You're up Sasha." Danny patted her on the back.

She hesitated at the doorway. "I need a minute." She backed up.

"Sasha..." Devin started.

"No...I just need a minute." She pressed backing up further.

"We don't have time for that," Devin said.

"Well make some." She said. "I am the one that has to do this, and I just need a second to breathe."

"Let me talk to her." Derek grabbed her hand and pulled her down the hall.

"We could die today," Sasha stated as soon as they were out of ear shot.

"Sasha." Derek started, but Sasha interrupted him.

"No, we might Derek...we might die today because of choices not our own." She wiped a stray tear away. "It's not fair that we have to do this, but we have to try right. We have to fix this otherwise we won't ever have a life that is our own. But," she shook her head. "I don't think I can do this..."

"No matter what happens when you walk through that door, I will protect you." He said firmly.

"You can't promise that." She argued.

"Yes I can," he cupped her face.

"Derek..." Sasha whispered staring up at him.

He leaned down letting his lips brush hers. Sasha closed her eyes and leaned into him. Derek deepened the kiss his hands wrapping around her waist.

"I will protect you," Derek said finally pulling back after a few seconds. He grabbed her hand and walked back to the group.

"Good?" Cassie asked once they were back.

Sasha nodded.

Devin placed his hand on the doorway, muttered the spell and the opening appeared. Derek, Danny, and Devin made a shield around them. Sasha took one last deep breath, calmed her emotions and walked through the opening.

The ballroom was beautifully decorated. Large tables filled the room. Each table filled with people Sasha had only dreamed of meeting in person. There was a dance floor in front of the table. In front of the dance floor was the head table. Her "father" Prince Alessandro and "grandparents" King Domenico and Queen Francesca sat there. She heard Devin close the opening behind them.

They were partially hidden by a drape, so no one had noticed them yet. The camera men were moving their cameras around the room to get the perfect view of everyone enjoying themselves. Sasha noticed that no one was on the dance floor. It seemed like the dinner portion just ended as the servants were clearing the tables.

"Now or never," Devin whispered.

Sasha stepped forward with everyone behind her. She made her way to the dance floor flanked by Derek and Danny, with Devin facing the crown. "Excuse me!" she yelled gathering the attention of those closest. She was immediately greeted with loud gasps as those who saw her realized who she was. As more people focused on the dance floor, the gasps grew louder.

Sasha capitalized on confusion and took the only chance she knew she would have. "My name is Sasha Delant and they…," She said as she pointed behind her to the Royal Family, "…are trying to kill me because I am the illegitimate daughter of Prince Alessandro, which makes me the Heir to Adalithiel!"

Chapter Forty

You could hear a pin drop in the hall after her announcement. All cameras were trained on her. She knew her window of opportunity was closing and she decided to capitalize on the silence and kept going.

"You can test my blood. I am his daughter. They are trying to cover it up by getting rid of everyone who knows the truth."

"Guards!" King Domenico yelled getting over his shock. "Seize her!"

Guard rushed forward, but the combined shield kept them at bay.

"Admit it!" She yelled as she turned to the King. "Admit that I am your granddaughter! Tell everyone the reason you are trying to kill me is that I am the next heir!"

"Stop your lies!" King Domenico hissed. "You are not of my blood!"

"Then test it!" She stared at him. "It's a very simple and quick test. We could find out right here in this room. Find out the truth in front of everyone."

There were murmurs around the hall. It was a simple test taking no longer than five minutes to prove.

Sasha turned back to the crowd. "They attacked us. Called my mother a murderer and arrested everyone who knew the truth because I am the illegitimate heir. He doesn't find me worthy of taking the crown one day even though I never knew about it or wanted it. My mother worked here at the castle, and she had an affair with Prince Alessandro. Once it was found out that she was pregnant by him, they took out her family, and she has been on the run. Please believe me." She pleaded. "Why would I come here if I was lying?"

"Guards!" King Domenico yelled once more red in the face.

"I am not attacking. I am not doing anything to harm him. I am just speaking the truth. The truth he worked so hard to cover up." She looked over the room. "We were living a quiet life until they attacked until they came after us."

"Why should we believe you?" a man in the crowd asked.

"Because I can prove it. You can do the test of my blood and of Prince Alessandro's and prove that I am his daughter. The world had no idea where I was, I had my chance to run and hide, but here I am trying to clear my family's name."

There were murmurs throughout the hall and Sasha could see people were considering her words.

"Enough, you are not a part of my family!" King Demenico yelled banging the table hard with his fist. "Your mother was a traitor who plotted against this family to take the throne, she-"

"-she is telling the truth," Alessandro said cutting off his father's rant. Gasps rang throughout the hall.

"What do you think you are doing?" The king turned to him. "Her mother plotted and schemed against us," he hissed.

"She is still my daughter." Alessandro stood. "I should have never gone along with this. These are not the actions of a Prince...or a father." He announced. "And I am going to fix that."

"Stop!" King Domenico yelled. "How dare you turn on your family!"

"I am not turning on my family. I'm

protecting them. Finally. You are a stubborn old fool who will not let go of his own prejudices. I will not allow you to harm my daughter or her mother and their family anymore. The world knows the truth." He gestured to the cameras with their blinking red lights.

The King glared at his son then up to his *granddaughter*. He shuttered at the word. He could not let that bloodline rule; he could not let the past works of his family go to waste over the truth. He glanced at the room, and he could see the minds changing in the guest. They were believing his son and the bastard girl. This could not happen; this was entirely their fault ... her fault.

With his eyes fixed on Sasha "I will never allow you to ruin this family's name!" he raised his hand creating a ball of fire and shot it at Sasha.

"No!" Alessandro yelled trying to stop the flame, but luckily their shield withstood the blast. "I will not allow you to harm my daughter." He came to stand in front of Sasha.

"She is a bastard!" King Domenico yelled.

"She is my child!" Alessandro retorted.

"And you have attacked an unarmed heir to the throne. You are refusing her birthright. You are trying to get rid of those who know the truth for your own selfish reason. You are not fit to be to be the ruler of this Kingdom."

Domenico's eyes widened at his son's words. "How dare you! This is treason!"

"I am doing what is best for this nation." Alessandro took a step towards his father. "I am not going to sit by and let you kill innocent people to further your misguided agenda." He cleared his throat. "I invoke order 10. I Prince Alessandro of Adalithiel here by announce King Domenico is not fit to rule for reasons known to this audience and now the Kingdom. As King, you have abused your power for personal reason and gain. You have imprisoned innocent people and killed countless members of this Kingdom to further your cause."

King Domenico stared down at his son in a rage. "How dare you invoke order 10...you ungrateful little boy..." he sputtered.

King Domenico looked around the room all eyes on him...many were not friendly. "I will not allow you to take this throne from me; order 10 be damned."

"You cannot refuse the order; it is up to the people to decide," said Prince Alessandro. "And I believe they have seen all they needed to see."

King Demenico stared at the men and women all staring at him in shock and anger. He turned to his wife. "And you what do you have to say!" he hissed.

"I am at the mercy of my people." She said keeping her composure "I will do what they ask of me."

"You all turn against me when it is in your best interest. I will not let my family's legacy fall and be tainted because you are all too weak." He raised his arms high, and red energy grew. "I would rather see this castle brought down to the ground than see you as part of this family."

"Stop this!" Alessandro yelled as guards came to his side to help him. "Father this is madness!"

"I will not allow that family to ruin all I have worked for! All my family has worked for!" He yelled, his hands continued to glow bright red. With a flick of his wrist flames grew around him and quickly circled the room.

"Father I am warning you!" Alessandro yelled again. The guards tried but failed to stop the growing flames.

"You warn me... *me*!" King Demenico yelled bringing the wall of flames up behind him. "I am King!" He yelled as he sent the wall towards the crowd. The hall erupted in screams as the flames danced towards them.

"Stop!" Sasha screamed as a blinding blue light shot out of her body encasing the room. Just like it had at her house the flames died the moment they encountered her magic.

"How?" King Demenico started in shock at her.

Sasha took a deep breath, the last of the flames going with them. "Because I'm royalty."

Alessandro quickly used his father's disbelief to his advantage and sent a small, but power, a ball of blue energy to his father. The guards were quick and placed a wizard necklace around his neck.

Alessandro walked up to his father. "I, Prince Alessandro, arrest you, King Demenico, for attacks against the crown... a crime punishable by death." The guards quickly escorted Demenico from the room.

…It was over. She fell back and felt Derek's arms wrap around her turning her to face him. "We did it." She smiled.

"No," he shook his head. "You did…I knew you could." He leaned down and placed a quick kiss on her lips before she was pulled from his grasp by Cassie.

"You did it!" She hugged her. "We are safe. You saved us!"

Epilogue

Sasha paced...today was the day...she was to be crowned the Princess of Adalithiel.

"You look beautiful honey." Her mother whispered kissing the side of her head careful not to mess up her hair. Jasmine was looking better these days. In the short few weeks, since she was taken out of the dungeons, she was on the road to making a full recovery. It was hard to believe the battered woman Sasha recused was the strong woman before her today.

"Thanks, Mom." Sasha blinked back tears.

"Sasha, it's time," Derek said from the door.

"Thanks," she nodded.

"I better go take my seat." Jasmine wiped a stray tear and gave Sasha one last kiss on her cheek before leaving the room. Jasmine took off to join Wendy, Danny, Devin, Cassie and her parents at their seats.

"See you out there," Sasha called after her. She looked around the room and thought about what was waiting for her out there. Her new life.

If you told her a few weeks ago, that she would be standing in the castle about to be crowned princess of Adalithiel, she would have laughed in your face. But here she was.

Sasha walked down the hall with Amie and Derek trailing behind her. She halted at the door to the hall where just a few weeks ago her "grandfather" tried to kill her. Now everyone in that room was there to see her be crowned their princess.

The doors opened, and with a deep breath, Sasha stepped forward to her future...

Epilogue

Alessandro walked down the quiet hall. He ran his hand along the long wall, pressing a few loose bricks along his way. He reached the end, and the wall slid open. He picked up the flashlight turned it on and walked down the narrow passage way until he reached the bottom. A small cage greeted him. He sneered at the occupant.

"Come for another visit?" The occupant asked from their bed. "Come to taunt me or to finally kill me?"

Alessandro snorted. "I have no reason to kill you. I told you this years ago; I need you alive to suffer."

"It's been close to seven years... I think I've suffered enough."

"That's where you're wrong." Alessandro shook his head. "Your suffering has just begun. I've won, she's here, and she's mine. They are **both** mine!" He relished as his prisoner's eyes widened.

"No." the prisoner whispered. "You're lying."

Alessandro reached into his pocket and

pulled out two locks of hair and tossed them into the cell. The prisoner fell to the floor and grabbed at the two locks of hair hugging them to their chest.

"No..." it was barely a whisper.

"Yes!" Alessandro smiled. "They are mine." He turned and started back up the narrow passage.

"Come back here!" The prisoner yelled. "Come back!"

Alessandro's laugh filled the narrow hallway as he walked away... it was good to be King.

ABOUT THE AUTHOR

ANDREA ROSE WASHINGTON loves all things fantasy, paranormal with a bit of mystery tossed in. She's never with without a book in her hand whether it is in print or e-book format. By day she is a mild manor woman with a Culinary Degree who works in the Hospitality Industry. By night she writes words that would make your head spin. If you want to know more about her life, follow her!

Twitter: AndreaRoseW
Tumblr:
http://andrearosewashington.tumblr.com/